A DREAM COME TRUE

Lucia opened her eyes with a start to find Lord Winterton standing in front of her. His horse was drinking from the river and he looked very handsome in his rust-coloured riding habit.

She jumped up as if she had been stung,

"Where are you going?" he asked, catching hold of her arm.

"I – I must return to the Hall. Mama – "

Lord Winterton stood there, still holding on to her arm. His blue eyes burned into her face and she noticed him lick his lips beneath his clipped moustache.

They remained staring into each other's eyes for a few seconds and then Lord Winterton suddenly pulled her towards him and his urgent mouth was on hers, kissing her in a manner she had never experienced.

She felt something inside of her soar before realising what she was doing.

"*No!*" she cried, pulling away – her face red and her head reeling from the kiss. "Let me go!"

THE BARBARA CARTLAND PINK COLLECTION

Titles in this series

A DREAM COME TRUE

BARBARA CARTLAND

Barbaracartland.com Ltd

THE BARBARA CARTLAND PINK COLLECTION

Barbara Cartland was the most prolific bestselling author in the history of the world. She was frequently in the Guinness Book of Records for writing more books in a year than any other living author. In fact her most amazing literary feat was when her publishers asked for more Barbara Cartland romances, she doubled her output from 10 books a year to over 20 books a year, when she was 77.

She went on writing continuously at this rate for 20 years and wrote her last book at the age of 97, thus completing 400 books between the ages of 77 and 97.

Her publishers finally could not keep up with this phenomenal output, so at her death she left 160 unpublished manuscripts, something again that no other author has ever achieved.

Now the exciting news is that these 160 original unpublished Barbara Cartland books are already being published and by Barbaracartland.com exclusively on the internet, as the international web is the best possible way of reaching so many Barbara Cartland readers around the world.

The 160 books are published monthly and will be numbered in sequence.

The series is called the Pink Collection as a tribute to Barbara Cartland whose favourite colour was pink and it became very much her trademark over the years.

The Barbara Cartland Pink Collection is published only on the internet. Log on to www.barbaracartland.com to find out how you can purchase the books monthly as they are published, and take out a subscription that will ensure that all subsequent editions are delivered to you by mail order to your home.

NEW

Barbaracartland.com is proud to announce the publication of ten new Audio Books for the first time as CDs. They are favourite Barbara Cartland stories read by well-known actors and actresses and each story extends to 4 or 5 CDs. The Audio Books are as follows :

The Patient Bridegroom	The Passion and the Flower
A Challenge of Hearts	Little White Doves of Love
A Train to Love	The Prince and the Pekinese
The Unbroken Dream	A King in Love
The Cruel Count	A Sign of Love

More Audio Books will be published in the future and the above titles can be purchased by logging on to the website www.barbaracartland.com or please write to the address below.

If you do not have access to a computer, you can write for information about the Barbara Cartland Pink Collection and the Barbara Cartland Audio Books to the following address :

Barbara Cartland.com Ltd.
Camfield Place,
Hatfield,
Hertfordshire AL9 6JE
United Kingdom.
Telephone:+44 (0)1707 642629
Fax:+44 (0)1707 663041

THE LATE DAME BARBARA CARTLAND

Barbara Cartland who sadly died in May 2000 at the age of nearly 99 was the world's most famous romantic novelist who wrote 723 books in her lifetime with worldwide sales of over 1 billion copies and her books were translated into 36 different languages.

As well as romantic novels, she wrote historical biographies, 6 autobiographies, theatrical plays, books of advice on life, love, vitamins and cookery. She also found time to be a political speaker and television and radio personality.

She wrote her first book at the age of 21 and this was called *Jigsaw*. It became an immediate bestseller and sold 100,000 copies in hardback and was translated into 6 different languages. She wrote continuously throughout her life, writing bestsellers for an astonishing 76 years. Her books have always been immensely popular in the United States, where in 1976 her current books were at numbers 1 & 2 in the B. Dalton bestsellers list, a feat never achieved before or since by any author.

Barbara Cartland became a legend in her own lifetime and will be best remembered for her wonderful romantic novels, so loved by her millions of readers throughout the world.

Her books will always be treasured for their moral message, her pure and innocent heroines, her good looking and dashing heroes and above all her belief that the power of love is more important than anything else in everyone's life.

"When lovers dream about love their dreams invariably come true."

Barbara Cartland

CHAPTER ONE
1913

"Do you, Serena Mary take this man – "

The bride was beautiful and everyone in the Church agreed that she looked a picture.

Although not in the first flush of youth, her eyes sparkled as brilliantly as the magnificent diamonds around her neck.

Her oyster-coloured silk dress was both fashionable and flattering for a woman of her age. The skirt was fitted to the hips and then hung straight down. The top was long-sleeved and covered in expensive lace.

'No! No!' thought Lucia, as she watched the happy couple gazing into each other's eyes and exchanging vows.

She had not wanted to come to this wedding and if there had been anything she could have done to prevent it happening, she would have.

'Mama, how could you?' she wanted to scream, trying not to cry. 'Papa has only been dead for a year and that man – *that man* was responsible.'

There were a few in the Church that day who would have not agreed with the first sentiment, if not the last.

The people of Shilborough were conservative and were still strict in their observance of mourning rituals and

Lady Serena Mountford had raised eyebrows when she had announced, barely eleven months after Lord Mountford's sad demise on the maiden voyage of *RMS Titanic* that she would marry for the second time.

"She is not even out of mourning," the villagers had gossiped, as she was driven past them in the family's sparkling Rolls Royce, still wearing the black woollen coat that marked her out as a widow. It had been Lord Mountford's pride and joy – a Silver Ghost – and one of the latest models.

Lord Mountford's Rolls Royce was one of the few motor cars to be found speeding around that part of Hertfordshire. Even more shocking, when alive, he had actually driven the vehicle himself, they muttered.

The Vicar continued the marriage ceremony and Lucia looked down at her bouquet of spring flowers that had been tied with a silk ribbon.

Had not they been quite content on their own without Sir Arthur McAllister?

She recalled the awful day when they had received the telegram from the family's Solicitor in London telling them of the sinking of the White Star ship en route to New York.

Lucia had been in the garden admiring the sea of daffodils that grew in undulating drifts across the rolling lawns of Bingham Hall.

How she loved the spring.

It was a beautiful afternoon. The birds were singing and Lucia was just contemplating changing into her riding habit, when a terrible howling noise, like an animal in pain, issued forth from the French windows that led to the drawing room, where her mother was doing her embroidery.

"Mama!" whispered Lucia alarmed. She ran back across the lawns as fast as her fashionably fitted skirt would allow her and threw open the glass doors.

Lady Mountford was on the sofa, rocking and sobbing, a discarded telegram lay at her feet while Moston, the butler, looked on horrified.

"Miss Lucia, thank Heaven," he murmured, as Lucia appeared.

"Mama! Mama! What is it?" she cried, throwing her arms around her mother's neck.

Lady Mountford could scarcely speak for crying. She tried to cover her face and simply pointed to the telegram on the floor.

"Oh, no – " muttered Lucia, as she picked it up.

"Please contact me urgently – stop – the RMS Titanic has sunk – stop – Lord Mountford not on first list of survivors – stop – Henry Urwin," it read.

Lucia's blood had run cold when she read the words in the telegram. Mr. Urwin was a friend as well as their Solicitor.

Both Lucia and her mother had been reluctant to allow Lord Mountford to travel to New York. He had invested in some factories in New York State on the advice of Sir Arthur McAllister, a business acquaintance of his.

Little did Lucia know as she sat there with the telegram in her shaking hand, what further part Sir Arthur was to play in their lives.

"Mama," she choked, trying to compose herself. "Have you telephoned Mr. Urwin?"

"Oh, Lucia, I cannot! What if he has not survived?"

"Mama, Mr. Urwin says that his name is not on the first list of survivors – that is not to say he has perished."

"Lucia, I had such misgivings about him going in the first place. It was as if I had a presentiment of disaster."

Lucia swallowed hard.

She must screw up her courage and telephone Mr.

Urwin. She had to.

"Moston, ask Bridget to bring Mama's *sal volatile* at once," she ordered in a clear calm voice.

"Very good, miss," he answered, unable to disguise his own emotions.

Moston had served Lord Mountford for many years and considered him a good employer. What would this turn of events mean for the servants of the Hall?

Lucia paced the drawing room floor and waited for Bridget to appear. Very soon she came into the room, carrying the small bottle of smelling salts that had been her mother's constant companion for many years.

Lady Mountford was of an extremely delicate constitution and it did not require much to induce a fit of the vapours. A sudden clap of thunder, a jolt of the carriage and even the servants had learned to make certain that she heard them entering a room, for fear of causing her to faint from shock.

Bridget fussed around her Mistress and talked soothingly to her.

"Come now, my Lady. Take a deep breath and inhale. You'll soon be feeling much better."

Lucia played with the tasselled ends of the lampshade and bit her lip. Could she summon up the courage to go into the hall and pick up the telephone?

She would have preferred to take the Rolls Royce to London to Mr. Urwin's office to see him in person, but she could not leave her mother.

Long moments passed and Lucia tried to still her heart that was beating so fast she felt as if it was leaping out of her chest.

Then calmly she walked into the hall.

The telephone had just been installed at the insistence

4

of her father, who was much concerned about her mother's health and Lucia thought it ironic that it was now he and not her mother who was the source of concern.

She picked up the earpiece, put it to her ear and after a short delay, the exchange answered,

"Yes, my Lady?"

"It is Miss Mountford here, Joyce," she said quietly, having recognised the voice of the operator. "Would you get me Chancery 212, please?"

"At once, Miss Mountford."

At last, she heard the voice of one of Mr. Urwin's clerks on the other end.

"Hello," she said loudly, as the line was a little faint. "Can I speak to Mr. Urwin, please? This is Miss Mountford of Shilborough calling."

The clerk put down the receiver and she waited anxiously until at last Mr. Urwin picked it up.

"Hello, Miss Mountford."

"Mr. Urwin. We received your telegram. Papa – "

"I am so very sorry to be the bearer of bad news, Miss Mountford. The first word we had of it was when we heard that they had sounded the Lutine Bell at Lloyd's. I expect there will be reports of it in the newspapers tomorrow. Terrible, terrible tragedy!"

"You said that Papa was not on the first list of survivors. Is there any further news?"

"I have one of my staff at the offices of the White Star Line now. He will come straight back as soon as there is anything to tell you. They are issuing lists of survivors as more reach dry land. He says that relatives have besieged the offices. Heaven only knows what it will be like by tomorrow when the reports hit the newspapers."

"But Papa – "

"My dear, there is every chance that he is safe. It would appear that what casualties there might be were largely crew and those who were in steerage and Second Class. The first survivors so far are nearly all First Class passengers."

Lucia hesitated – she had been on steam ships before and she had read stories of disasters at sea. Was not the cry *women and children first*?

"Were there any male survivors in the first bulletins?" she asked hesitantly.

There was a long pause and Lucia's heart was gripped by a black fear. Her throat contracted.

Finally Mr. Urwin replied,

"Very few. I did not wish to alarm you unduly but, at the same time, I wished you to know before you read it in the newspapers. It is still morning on the East coast of America and no doubt we shall hear more later on."

Lucia thanked him and put down the receiver, a million thoughts teeming through her head.

'If anything has happened to Papa, I shall never forgive Sir Arthur McAllister for sending him to his doom,' she decided, as she walked to the drawing room.

Her mother was lying on the sofa propped up with pillows. Bridget was fussing over her still and trying to get her to drink a glass of brandy.

"Just a nip, my Lady. It will help to soothe your nerves."

Lady Mountford opened her eyes and saw Lucia in the doorway.

"Lucia!" she cried, "what did he say?"

"There is no news of him, Mama. But Mr. Urwin says that not all survivors have reached land yet. As soon as he has any news, he will be in touch."

"I do not think I would survive the shock if he has – "

"Hush, Mama. While there is no definite news, there is hope."

But in her heart Lucia felt nothing. She knew in her bones that her father had perished.

*

There had followed agonising weeks while Lucia tended to her prostrate mother and they waited anxiously for news. And then, on April 30th, Mr. Urwin made the journey from Holborn to Shilborough to deliver the sad tidings.

"He died a hero," he said, as Lady Mountford dissolved into tears comforted by a weeping Lucia.

"It appears that Lord Mountford had given up his place on one of the lifeboats in order that a Second Class woman with a child could take his seat. His body was recovered from the sea and identified through a letter in his wallet."

"Will we have to travel to America to bring him home?" asked Lucia, composing herself whilst her mother wailed beside her. "Mama would not hear of him being buried in an American cemetery. There have been reports in the newspapers that some are to be buried in Nova Scotia or at sea."

"The body will be shipped back to England in the next few weeks," advised Mr. Urwin, his face as grey as ash.

Mr. Urwin had been as good as his word. A few weeks later, Lord Mountford arrived back home at Bingham Hall.

At the funeral, some days afterwards, Lucia stood mute before the same altar where she now stood, watching her mother marry the man whom she held responsible for her father's untimely death.

'I hate him! I hate him!' she told herself, as the Reverend Brown concluded the service. 'If it were not for him and his stupid schemes, Papa would be alive today.'

"I now pronounce you, man and wife."

Sir Arthur leaned forward and kissed his new wife on the cheek. The organ swelled into life, but Lucia was not listening.

She simmered with resentment as the new Lady McAllister walked down the aisle smiling and happy.

Lucia could see that some of the congregation were far from smiling. Many of the relatives who now gathered in the Church had disapproving looks on their faces. Could they, too, be remembering that it was only the previous year that they had gathered here to witness her father's funeral?

'Surely Mama could not have forgotten Papa already?' thought Lucia, as they emerged into the spring sunshine. 'We are but a few steps away from his grave.'

But the new Lady McAllister did not cast so much as a glance at the imposing tomb to the right of the Church door.

'I wish it had rained,' she fumed, as her mother and stepfather approached the immaculate Rolls Royce specially decorated for the occasion. A new chauffeur, Briggs, held open the door for them and saluted as they climbed in.

'And all these new staff,' she groaned. 'There was no need to employ a chauffeur. Jack, the head groom, is perfectly adequate.'

But she knew that by bringing in new staff, Sir Arthur was asserting his authority. It galled her that he would now be in charge of Bingham Hall, where the Mountfords had always been the Lords and Masters. But Lucia did not have any brothers or sisters, and, given her mother's age, it was unlikely that she would.

'I should be grateful for that, I suppose,' she thought, as she climbed into a smart white landau. It had been hired for the occasion, a statement to the people of Shilborough that Sir Arthur was a force to be reckoned with in his own right.

Lucia watched as the Rolls Royce growled into life. She wondered what it might be like to be behind the wheel. Would it, she wondered, be as exciting as being on Starlight as he galloped across the hills?

The route back to the Hall took them through the village. If the happy couple had expected the villagers to throng the streets and cheering, they were mistaken.

A few surly people watched as the car purred down the main street. Many were simply curious to see the vehicle, as it was such a rare sight. Small children ran after it, shouting with delight, but they were the only ones with smiling faces.

'They all think that Mama has been foolish,' thought Lucia, as she gripped the sides of the open-topped carriage.

Bingham Hall had been a hive of activity since the early hours of the morning. The servants had had little or no sleep as preparations began for the lavish meal that was to be held in the ballroom.

There was a marquee erected in the garden, so that guests might wander outside and look at the daffodils and primroses. Lucia thought bitterly of how in the previous spring she had been enjoying them just before her world fell apart.

After Lord Mountford's funeral, her mother had become bedridden with an illness that any number of doctors seamed unable to cure.

Specialists from Harley Street made the journey to Bingham Hall, one after the other, leaving expensive bills in their wake.

Lucia had been forced to take charge of the accounts, but it was all new to her and she did not understand how the books worked.

It did not feel right dealing with her father's bank and so when the letter came informing them that no more cheques would be honoured until more funds were placed in the account, she did not know where to turn.

Thankfully Henry Urwin had proved to be a rock and soon afterwards her mother began to show signs of improvement. During those long days, Sir Arthur McAllister became a frequent visitor to the Hall.

At first, Lucia could not believe that her mother received him, but when Sir Arthur said that he wished to discuss her father's business affairs with her, Lucia could not object.

She was very mindful of the letters arriving from the bank that she now forwarded to Mr. Urwin.

Something told her that perhaps things were not right, but until the day that Mr. Urwin told her as much, she ignored her suspicions.

*

"Lucia, how lovely you look."

Lucia was jolted from her thoughts by the voice of Geoffrey Charlton, the brother of one of her dearest friends, Emmeline.

Geoffrey took her hand and kissed it.

"You look as if you are rather cold," he observed. "The landau was probably not the best idea in the middle of March!"

Lucia laughed.

She was enormously fond of Geoffrey although she would never think of him as anything other than Emmeline's naughty little brother.

"Yes, I am rather chilly," replied Lucia. "I will ask Moston to bring me a warmer wrap."

"It was a lovely service, wasn't it? Your Mama looked beautiful."

"Geoffrey, you are not usually so tactful."

"It is not for me to pass comment on such hasty nuptials," added Geoffrey mischievously.

"You just have," answered Lucia. "Now, come, take me into the ballroom, please. Otherwise I shall be waylaid by one of Sir Arthur's cronies."

"He is from the North, is he not?"

"Yes, Manchester," replied Lucia, as they made their way to the ballroom. "He owns a factory there, but also has investments in America and South Africa."

"With such a name, he must have Scottish ancestry?"

"I believe so, although it is a long way back. Mama was rather vague about it when I asked her."

"I do believe I can see a tinge of red in that beard," commented Geoffrey with a wry smile, "so I would say that he is definitely part-Scotch!"

Lucia was happy that Geoffrey had come to the wedding as Emmeline had been forced to stay at home with a bad cold that had already lasted a week.

"Walk with me to my table, Geoffrey, do be a dear," urged Lucia, as they were ushered into the magnificent ballroom, which had been decorated lavishly and the tables were groaning with silver candelabra and bowls of flowers.

"Mama was up half the night arranging them," pointed out Lucia. "She insisted on doing as many of the floral arrangements as possible even though she knows her health might suffer. It's one of her hobbies."

Lucia arrived at the top table where her mother and stepfather were already seated. Her mother smiled brilliantly at her and patted the chair next to hers.

"You are here, darling, and Geoffrey, you are on the table with my sister."

Geoffrey smiled politely and bade Lucia a temporary

farewell.

As she sank down into her chair, she wished that he could have stayed with her. Instead, her dining companion was her deaf Great-Uncle Hubert. He had made the journey from London and seemed thoroughly bemused that his niece was getting married for the second time.

"A man needs a wife!" he boomed. "I myself have been married three times, but no lady will have an old man like me now."

Lucia thought that he must be seventy-five if he was a day and sympathised with him over the lack of suitable companions.

"I don't care to take a young wife," he continued, as the first course was served. "I prefer a more mature woman."

Lucia found herself smiling, even though she knew he did not mean to be amusing.

All through the five-course banquet, Lucia watched her new stepfather.

He was tall and well-built without being corpulent and his face was neither unattractive nor handsome. His brown hair was greying and he wore a full beard that gave him a somewhat nautical appearance.

'It was a pity it was not him on board the *Titanic*,' she fumed darkly, as he laughed gaily with her mother. 'Why can Mama not see through him? He must have been thrilled to acquire yet another property for the great McAllister empire.'

Even though he boasted a title, Lucia knew that it was only a Knighthood. He stood to gain a great deal, she believed, by being associated with the Mountford family.

The thought suddenly struck her. What would happen to her if her mother died? Would she be penniless? Surely, her mother would not leave the house and what money remained to her new husband?

Lucia fell silent as she pondered her fate. She wished she did not have to be there at all pretending to smile when she felt so utterly miserable.

After the long meal had finished, Lucia made her excuses and went upstairs to change her clothes. Her maid, Mary-Anne, was waiting with her ball gown ready and pressed.

Much as Lucia would have liked to have feigned a headache and remained in her room, she knew that she could not.

"Her Ladyship looks so happy!" sighed Mary-Anne, as she dressed Lucia's hair. "It will feel odd to have a new Master in the house, won't it?"

"He will never replace my Papa," she muttered grimly.

Blushing, Mary-Anne realised she had spoken out of turn.

"I'm sorry, miss. I did not mean to offend."

"Do not concern yourself, Mary-Anne. The Hall is still Mama's by rights and, even if she has changed her name, she is still a Mountford."

"Yes, miss."

Mary-Anne put the finishing touches to Lucia's coiffeur in silence. If the truth were told, she did not care for the look of the new Master and neither did many of the servants at the Hall. They considered him to be a jumped-up trader who was seeking to better himself.

The servants of Bingham Hall were rather old-fashioned in their views and were proud to be working for members of the aristocracy. Some felt that Sir Arthur might lower the tone of the place.

By the time that Lucia came downstairs, the ballroom had been cleared for dancing. Guests had spilled out into the marquee in the garden and she could hear the musicians tuning up.

Lucia spotted Geoffrey Charlton coming through into the ballroom. She walked quickly over to him.

"Lucia. How can you be yet more dazzling than earlier?"

"Geoffrey, you should save your chatter for someone who will believe it," she retorted smiling.

"Come now, if I cannot practise my flattery on my dear sister's charming friend – "

"Geoffrey, you must promise me that you will take the first dance with me. I don't want one of my stepfather's dreadful friends to think they have the right."

"It will be my pleasure, but Lucia, dearest, do I detect a hint of dislike for your new stepfather?"

"You know that I hold him responsible for Papa's death," she replied, giving him a cold stare. "If it were not for him and his stupid investment schemes, Papa would still be here."

Geoffrey sighed and took Lucia's hand.

"And who is to say that your father would not have died in that blasted car of his he insisted on driving himself? My dear, I believe that when the Almighty decrees that it is time for us to join him, then join him we must!"

"That is a very fatalistic view of life, Geoffrey."

"Nevertheless, you should try and comfort yourself with that thought, dark though it might seem. But I do understand why you might not welcome him into the bosom of your family – he is not one of us, is he?"

"No, Geoffrey, he is not. But we should not hold it against him that his grandfather was a dyer. He worked very hard to own the textiles factory where he was originally employed – "

The handsome young man looked slightly scornful and

then remembered that Lucia was a modern soul who did not look down on the working classes.

"You will be telling me next that you agree with these Suffragette women," he sneered, as they took their place at the edge of the dance floor.

"I believe that married women should have the vote. Do we not, after all, give birth to men?"

Geoffrey laughed.

"No doubt, you wished you could have been there, lighting the fuse that nearly blew up Lloyd George's house the other week?"

Their political argument was interrupted by the orchestra's first few notes. It ran through Geoffrey's mind that Lucia, if she was not careful, would find it most difficult to find a husband herself, if she continued to express such radical views.

He looked at her as he took her in his arms to dance – she was very beautiful with her pretty blonde hair and wistful grey eyes. She was intelligent and amusing with many accomplishments. But her opinions –

'If only they were not so forthright and so damned unfeminine!' he thought.

Lucia was unaware of what was going through Geoffrey's mind. She had no conceit about her attractiveness, but did not consider herself especially lovely.

Her mother had been a great beauty in her day, which was one of the reasons that Lord Mountford had fallen in love with her and, even now, Lucia felt that she outshone many women far younger than herself.

She watched as her mother and Sir Arthur whirled around the room to the Viennese waltz. So elegant and majestic.

'If Mama had not been so ill after Papa died, she

would not have been so weak as to have fallen prey to his attentions.' she mused, feeling sick inside each time her mother smiled at Sir Arthur.

The dance came to and end and Lucia told Geoffrey that she wished to sit the next one out.

"I am feeling a little unwell," she said. "I am not used to so much champagne so early in the day."

She was just about to leave the floor, when she felt a tap on her shoulder.

Turning around, she saw it was Sir Arthur.

"Lucia. As my new stepdaughter, I hope you will do me the honour of having this dance with me."

Lucia opened her mouth to protest, but over Sir Arthur's shoulder she saw her mother urging her to accept.

With a curt nod of her head, she allowed him to lead her onto the floor.

"Your dress suits you well," he said, as he moved in time to the music whilst holding her stiffly. "It's French silk, is it not?"

"From Bond Street, yes."

"And I'll wager you paid far too much for it. Tch! London prices! The shopkeepers know that silly London fools will pay over the odds and push up their prices accordingly."

Lucia tried to ignore his comments. She feared, if she replied, she would sound irritated.

"You know that I now regard you as my own daughter," he continued, "and as such, I will provide the correct guidance for you. Without a man's superior knowledge, it's too easy for women to fall prey to idle indulgence."

"Papa always used to praise me for my sensible and practical nature."

"What in buying over-priced gowns in Bond Street? Pah!"

A hot surge of anger rose up inside Lucia. How dare this man pass comment on her father? Who did he think he was?

"No, Lucia, I am your Guardian now and man of the house and I will expect you, as my dutiful stepdaughter, to follow my rules and not your father's."

Lucia stopped dancing and stared at him.

"Sir, I must retire at once, I declare I feel quite unwell."

Without waiting for a response, Lucia quickly left the dance floor. Before she had even reached the door, her mother was at her side.

"Lucia, what on earth possessed you to behave in such a rude fashion? You have offended Arthur."

"And is it acceptable for him to make offensive comments about Papa to me? Mama, do not ask me to listen gladly whilst he criticises my own father!"

"Darling, I know this is difficult for you."

"Mama, why did you have to marry him so soon after Papa's death? Do you care nothing for what people are saying?"

"Lucia, I am still your mother and you shouldn't speak to me like this," she snapped, tears welling up in her eyes. "Come outside. Everyone is looking at us."

She took Lucia into the library and closed the door.

With tears running down her face, she took her daughter's hand.

"Darling, I want you to understand. If it had not been for Sir Arthur, we would both be out on the street."

"What do you mean?" asked Lucia, her voice trembling.

"My long illness was an expensive one and your father made some very ill-advised investments shortly before he died. I know it has come to your attention that there is not much money in the bank, but what you do not know is that had I not married Sir Arthur then Mr. Urwin advised me that we would have to sell Bingham Hall and live in reduced circumstances!"

"No! It cannot be," answered Lucia horrified.

Her mother was now weeping freely.

"It's true. Our funds were so low that Mr. Urwin suggested that I begin to sell off some of our belongings – I was forced as well to take – certain steps. Sir Arthur was such a comfort to me during those dark days and then, when he proposed, I agreed to marry him. Darling, he loves me very much. You must accept him, as I have done and be nice to him."

All the resentment towards him bubbled up inside Lucia and she began to cry.

How could her mother ask such a thing of her? She had made no mention of loving the man, so why should she obey him as if he was her own father?

She tried to control her emotions.

It was almost as if someone, or something, else had taken her over – words came out of her mouth without her bidding and she found herself running away, out of the library and towards the garden.

'No! I would rather end up a pauper in the workhouse than have him as my stepfather!' she wept, blinded by tears as she, without thinking, made her way to the Rolls Royce that stood in the drive.

CHAPTER TWO

"Richard – do you have to go?"

The striking-looking woman with the curly red hair pulled the bed covers up to her chin and pouted as the tall handsome man with the thick brown hair and piercing blue eyes leapt out from between the sheets and pulled on his shirt.

She eyed his muscular frame and sighed.

Lord Winterton was as superb a lover as he was at everything else he turned his attentions to. And now, after such a short visit, he was leaving.

"Now, Camilla, you knew that I had an important appointment this afternoon and that I could only stay a few hours. I told you as soon as I arrived."

"But, darling – "

"Camilla, please do not look at me like that."

She was gazing pleadingly up at him from the warmth of her bed – the bed that she had once shared with her husband, Lord Shelley, who had died when he fell off his horse the previous September.

Lord Winterton never failed to find it amusing that he was cocking a snook at the man he called 'the old boy' up in Heaven.

She mustered every last inch of seductiveness as she

patted the space beside her.

"I have to go," he told her curtly, buttoning up his jacket and looking for his gloves. Although it was early March, there was quite a nip in the air.

He walked over to the bed and kissed her on top of her mass of red curls.

Somehow he had found himself seeing rather more of her than he had intended, now that certain other matters brought him more often to London.

Before leaving the boudoir, he took one last look at himself in Lady Shelley's cheval mirror. He was presentable enough for the appointment ahead.

He smoothed his clipped moustache into place and then, bade Camilla farewell without turning around.

"But when will I see you again?" she called to his departing back.

Hearing the front door slam shut, she snorted with anger and, picking up one of the feather pillows next to her, hurled it at the bedroom door.

"Cad!" she hissed, curling her pretty mouth into a sneer. "Perhaps I will not be at home the next time you come to call."

*

Outside Bingham Hall, Lucia sat in the empty car and sobbed her heart out for half an hour. She was only too familiar with the fate of fictional heroines when their mothers remarried and wondered if a similar one awaited her.

'The way he spoke to me,' she whispered, as she dried her eyes with her handkerchief. 'How dare he? If I had a brother, I would have had him call him outside, or at least, have words with him.'

But Lucia did not have a brother to share her burden.

Furthermore, what her mother had just told her had

shocked her to the core.

'Could Papa really have landed us in such dire straits?' she said to herself. 'It hardly seems possible. He always seemed such a wise and careful man when it came to money.'

She noticed that a footman was approaching the car.

She quickly composed herself and tucked away her handkerchief.

"Is everything all right, Miss Mountford?" he asked.

"Y-yes, thank you. I just wanted to be alone for a moment or two," she murmured, stepping out of the car as he held the door open.

She looked quickly around the drive and could not see anyone who might know her, so she ran back indoors shivering.

'And now I feel terribly guilty for upsetting her so much,' she thought gloomily. 'It was wrong of me to do so on her wedding day.'

She walked quickly towards the library but her mother was not there.

'No doubt, she will be with her guests,' she thought and went off to find her.

"Darling. There you are."

Lucia had just entered the ballroom when her mother came up behind her.

"Mama, I'm sorry – "

"Ssh. We shall not speak about it again today. I am glad I have found you because I will shortly be going upstairs to change."

"You are leaving already?"

"Arthur has booked us on the midnight train. We are going on the Orient Express all the way to Venice, did I not tell you?"

Lucia hung her head.

She now felt utterly wretched at her behaviour. The day was not meant to be about her. It was her mother's day.

"You will have a wonderful time," sighed Lucia. "Now, don't you worry about me, Geoffrey has been looking after me. Look, there he is, waving at us."

They returned his salutation and Lucia kissed her mother's cheek.

"I will come and see you off when you are ready to leave," she whispered, as Geoffrey made his way towards them. "I want you to be extremely happy and enjoy a fabulous honeymoon."

"What ho, Lucia!" called Geoffrey. "I thought you had run off."

"No, I have come to my senses," she answered thoughtfully. "I shall try to make the best of the situation."

"Dashed right, old girl," he replied heartily. "And I think a dance is the order of the day, wouldn't you?"

Lucia took his proffered arm and laughed, allowing him to lead the way.

'I will try and be happy for Mama,' she told herself, as Geoffrey swung her around the dance floor.

*

They were gone for three weeks and Lucia made the most of enjoying her time alone in Bingham Hall.

After the clearing up, she wrote herself out a list of things to do and set about organising the redecoration of her bedroom, but once the decorators had moved in, she became bored and listless.

She wandered outside into the grounds and eventually, found herself by the new timber garage that had been built to house the Rolls Royce Silver Ghost.

Briggs had brought the vehicle outside and was

washing it.

"Good afternoon, miss," he said, touching his cap with his soapy hand and leaving suds dripping from it.

Lucia laughed out loud.

"Hallo, Briggs. Now, look what I have made you do!"

"That's all right, miss. A bit of soap and water doesn't hurt. I thought I'd clean the car as there is nothing much to do while the Master's away."

Lucia walked around the wet car and inspected the leather seats and acres of chrome. She ran her hand along the carriage work as an audacious idea occurred to her.

"Briggs, would you teach me to drive this car?" she asked, half expecting him to shoo her away.

He put down his sponge and looked at her.

"Well, you're the boss while the Master's away, miss. If you order me to teach you to drive, then I must obey. He said I was to do as you said in his absence."

Lucia almost hugged herself with delight. She had longed to sit behind the wheel, but had never found the right opportunity – and now, this was it!

"Let me run inside and put on a hat and gloves. Briggs, will it be very breezy? Will we be going very fast?"

"That depends on you, miss," he replied with a cheeky smile.

It took her some time to find her gloves but, soon, she was running down the stairs and out through the front door where Briggs had brought the Rolls Royce.

"Hop inside and I'll show you the controls," he said. "This is the steering wheel and you turn it left to go left and right to go right. That's the accelerator – push gently on it to go forward. But first, you put it in gear, like so – "

Lucia screamed with joy as she took off the handbrake, released the clutch and the car moved forwards.

"Show me again how to change gear," she cried.

"You're a very fast learner, miss, for a young lady," he said in awe.

They practised until she heard the gong sound for afternoon tea, but she was too excited to do more than drink a cup of Earl Grey.

'How thrilling!' she said to herself, as she looked forward to her next lesson with Briggs. 'Very soon, I shall be able to visit all my friends and show off what a fine driver I am.'

And so, Lucia spent the rest of the week practising as much as she could. Briggs showed her how to pull up the hood and how to fill it with petrol.

Very soon, she was speeding along the drive and out onto the country roads.

"I can see I shall have to put in extra pins" she cried, one day after almost losing her hat in a hedgerow.

"I think you're ready to go out on your own," suggested Briggs, "but mind you be careful with it. This here Silver Ghost is the only one for miles around and Sir Arthur will blame me if anything happens to it."

"It was my father's car," countered Lucia, quietly prickling at the mention of Sir Arthur's name.

"Sorry, miss. I didn't know that," replied Briggs embarrassed. "The Master led me to believe that it was his car."

Lucia fell silent as they returned to the Hall.

'Is there anything that he has not laid claim to?' she fumed to herself.

*

A few days later it was bright and sunny and so Lucia put on her gloves and hat and ran out to the garage. Briggs was in the stables chatting to Jack and he soon broke off his conversation to drive the Rolls Royce out of the garage.

'I shall surprise Emmeline,' she said to herself, as the engine warmed up.

Lucia thrilled as she drove along the lanes with the wind tugging at her hair.

She was soon driving through the gates of the Grange, where Emmeline and Geoffrey lived and she could not wait to see their faces as she bowled up in the car.

Outside the front door she tooted the horn noisily as Briggs had shown her.

The Charlton's butler came rushing out and his face broke into a wry smile.

"Meek, would you mind bringing Miss Charlton out to the car, please? I want to surprise her!"

The butler nodded and disappeared back inside, only to bring a puzzled Emmeline out to the car five minutes later.

"Goodness," she cried. "I thought poor Meek had taken leave of his senses when he said I was to come outside. And now, I can see why. Did you really drive over here all on your own? Are you certain that your chauffeur is not hiding in the bushes and this is some joke?"

Lucia laughed.

"No, Emmeline. Briggs is responsible for teaching me. Is Geoffrey at home? Do run and fetch him."

"No, he is out, but I do have guests who have come for coffee. Please come and join us. I am certain that they will find your new skill most interesting."

Lucia jumped out of the car and dusted off her jacket. Emmeline took her friend by the hand and led her into the morning room.

"Everyone, I want you to meet my very dear friend, Miss Lucia Mountford. She has driven over here in a motor car, all on her own. What do you think of that?"

Emmeline had a look of triumph upon her face, knowing what kind of kudos this would lend to her by proxy. Very few people in the County owned cars and not only did she know someone who did, but she also drove it herself!

"This is Cecily Armstrong, and her sister, May. That gentleman by the piano is Lord Hornby's youngest son, Tristram."

Lucia shook hands with them all and then blushed, as her eyes met those of a rather good-looking young man who had just moved forwards. He was tall and slender with neat black hair and friendly hazel eyes.

"Lucia, this is Edward de Redcliffe," said Emmeline with a smile.

It had not escaped her notice that he could not stop staring at her friend.

"We have not met before," began Lucia, as she shook his hand.

"I think I would have remembered, had we done so," he replied with a warm smile.

"I am sorry that Geoffrey is not here to witness your great surprise," said Emmeline. "He is in London today buying books for his new job."

"When does he start?"

"A week on Monday. I think earning an honest day's crust will come as a complete shock to him after gadding about Italy and France for so long."

"Dear old Geoffrey," interjected Tristram. "I give him a month, tops!"

Lucia sat down and at once Edward de Redcliffe came and sat beside her.

"You are a very brave young lady," he remarked. "Driving a motor vehicle."

"It is – was my father's," she answered, correcting

herself quickly. "Mama and my stepfather are on honeymoon at the moment and I found myself with time on my hands, so I asked the chauffeur to teach me how to drive."

"So, do you live nearby, Miss Mountford?" asked Edward in his quiet voice.

"Yes, quite nearby. At Bingham Hall."

"Ah, I do not know it. I live in Mayfair mainly, but my parents have a house just outside Hertford."

"Then that is not too far away," replied Lucia, thinking that she might care to see Edward de Redcliffe again.

"You must come to the Hall for tea with Emmeline."

She blushed as she spoke, hoping that she was not sounding as if she was being too forward.

As they chattered, she noticed that Edward seemed to prefer to listen, rather than join in. Although with both Tristram and Cecily dominating the conversation, it would have taken a forceful soul to make his presence felt.

"Well, I must be going," announced Lucia eventually, as the clock in the hall struck midday. "With Mama and my stepfather away, it has fallen to me to be in charge and there is so much to be done."

She went round to everyone in turn and shook their hands.

"It was very nice to meet you," she said firmly, as she lingered over her goodbyes to Edward.

"Let me walk you to your motor car," he offered.

Outside he closed the car door behind her and admired the Silver Ghost.

"It's a fine vehicle. They say it is the best on earth."

Lucia chuckled.

"I could not possibly make that judgement as it is the only motor vehicle I have ever been in."

"Miss Mountford, might I call on you tomorrow?"

Lucia blushed with pleasure. She felt a surge of excitement, as if her life was really beginning again.

"Yes, I would like that very much. Come for afternoon tea at three o'clock. I shall make certain that cook bakes one of her fine coconut cakes."

"Until tomorrow," he called, waving as she pulled off down the drive.

*

When Lucia returned to the Hall, she noticed a telegram in amongst the pile of letters on the desk in the study. She picked it up, at first fearing it was for her, but then she saw that it was addressed to her stepfather.

She put it back down at once, remembering only too clearly the day that the telegram had arrived from Mr. Urwin.

'I hope it is not bad news,' she mused, suddenly filled with the urge to go upstairs to where she had erected a small shrine to her father.

Leaving the study, she ran up the stairs to the tiny alcove where a candle always burned next to a photograph of Lord Mountford.

'I wonder if my stepfather will have this removed once he returns?' she thought, as she stroked her father's face.

'They say that he had his house in Manchester razed to the ground and a new one built before he would occupy it. If he has such a mania for change, might he not attempt to do the same at Bingham Hall?'

Lucia lit another candle and placed it in a vacant holder and she prayed fervently to her father,

'If you have any influence up in Heaven, please, Papa, do not let Sir Arthur change one little thing at Bingham Hall.'

She turned her face Heavenwards and prayed hard and long until her knees began to ache.

'If I can do anything to prevent change at the Hall, then I shall,' she resolved, getting up. 'Papa, I swear it to you!'

*

The next afternoon, as promised, Edward de Redcliffe arrived at Bingham Hall on horseback.

They went for a ride together and Lucia felt very much as if their conversation consisted of a list of questions designed to ascertain whether or not she would make a suitable wife.

On returning, she had the distinct impression that she had discounted herself by expressing sentiments that he could instantly label as Suffragette.

She thought she would hear no more from him, but a few days later a note arrived asking her to a grand ball to be held at a mutual friend's house the following week.

She accepted in writing and then threw herself into preparing the Hall for her mother's return that weekend.

The return of the McAllisters to Bingham Hall was greeted by a flurry of activity. The servants all lined up outside as the Rolls Royce drew up by the front door.

Moston led a half-hearted cheer as Sir Arthur climbed out of the car, while everyone seemed delighted to see her mother again.

Lucia ran towards her and was swept up in her arms.

"Mama, you look so very well!"

"I feel wonderful, darling. Venice was a complete tonic although I must confess to a slight cough that developed whilst we were there. A doctor, however, assured me that it is nothing."

Lucia linked arms with her as they walked into the Hall.

" Moston has tea ready in the drawing room and I want to hear all about your trip."

She noticed that Sir Arthur had walked straight into the study. She wondered how he would react to the telegram awaiting him and was curious as to what news it contained.

In the drawing room Lucia and her mother had not been talking for long when he entered the room with a look on his face that confirmed Lucia's suspicions.

"Serena," he said with a look on his face like thunder. "I wish to see you alone at once. Lucia, please make yourself scarce."

Feeling hurt, Lucia arose from her chair and left the room.

'Why could he not speak while I was in the room? I am no longer a child.'

The April sunshine enticed her outside and so, she wandered out into the garden to stretch her legs.

After a while, she could not contain her curiosity. She was close to the French windows of the drawing room and she could see inside if she moved a little nearer.

But her stealth was not well rewarded.

'Mama. She is crying! It must indeed be bad news as she was in such good spirits when she arrived. Oh, I do hope that she will not become ill with the strain.'

After whiling away a nervous half-hour in the garden, Lucia could bear it no longer.

'I cannot wait until someone deigns to tell me what is going on,' she said to herself, feeling upset at the way her stepfather was treating her.

But as she entered the Hall, Moston came towards her.

"Ah, Miss Lucia, I was about to look for you. The Master wishes to see you at once in the study."

She did not waste any time and made her way to the study without hesitating.

It felt odd knocking on the door, knowing that it would

be Sir Arthur sitting there, not her father.

"Come in!"

Lucia could tell at once by his curt tone that he was not in a good humour.

"Lucia, please sit down."

Sir Arthur did not meet her gaze. He stood behind the large oak desk and addressed himself to the pile of papers stacked in front of him.

"Lucia, you will no doubt have seen a telegram arrive whilst we were away. It does not bring good news. The short of it is that the American factory in which I invested has gone into liquidation, leaving considerable debts in its wake. If I cannot find twenty-five thousand pounds at once, then I shall lose everything – the factory in Manchester and, most likely, we shall have to sell Bingham Hall."

"No! You cannot! It is Mama's."

"It is the *bank's*, Lucia, not your mother's. She was forced to mortgage it after your father died and that is why we need so much money to bail ourselves out."

Lucia was dumbstruck. Sell Bingham Hall? That could not happen!

Just then, her mother entered the room. All the bloom had drained from her cheeks and her eyes were puffy from crying.

"Oh, my dear. I am so sorry," she wailed rushing to Lucia's side. "I have already told you how my long illness and the expense of settling your father's debts had plunged us into debt. I did not tell you at the time, but I had to mortgage Bingham Hall to make ends meet. So, now there is no spare money."

Lucia looked up miserably at her mother and then at Sir Arthur, who stood at his desk fuming, as if it had somehow been Lord Mountford's fault that he was now in danger of bankruptcy.

'How dare he look injured, when it is all his fault that we now find ourselves in such dreadful circumstances after persuading Mama to marry him off the back of his so-called fortune!'

She wished she could voice her feelings and may indeed have done, had her mother not presented such a pathetically sad figure beside her. She was crying again and wringing her hands.

"What is to become of us? What is to become of us?" she repeated over and over again.

"As I said to your mother," continued Sir Arthur, "it may come to pass that I shall have to sell everything I own down South and then, we will have to move to my home in Didsbury."

"Move up North?" cried Lucia horrified. "That would mean us leaving all we have known in Shilborough – and London! Mama, you cannot agree to this."

"Darling, we might not have the choice," said her mother in a wan voice. "If your stepfather cannot raise the money, you will have to face the fact that we shall have to move."

Lucia sat in her chair feeling numb and shocked. She had not expected anything so dreadful.

'Leave Bingham Hall?' she wailed to herself, as her mother continued to cry softly. Just when she had believed her life to be starting anew comes this ghastly piece of news.

'Leave Shilborough for some dirty Northern town I will hate? Never! *Never!*'

CHAPTER THREE

A pall of misery hung over Bingham Hall for the next few days. Lucia scarcely saw Sir Arthur who spent much of his time closeted in the study with dour-looking men who had the slightly earnest air of accountants.

Lucia became accustomed to dining alone with her mother, as his meetings went on long into the evening.

She became very concerned about the change that had come over her mother during this time. The healthy complexion she had brought back from Italy soon vanished and often she took to her bed for hours at a time.

The cough that she had dismissed as being 'slight' became more pronounced and Lucia could hear it echoing along the corridors late at night.

She pushed her food around her plate at mealtimes and said she was not hungry. Lucia kept a close eye upon her, fearing that her old illness might recur.

She almost telephoned Edward de Redcliffe to ask him to take someone else to the ball, but her mother would not hear of it.

"You must go and keep your stepfather company," she insisted, sitting up in bed one afternoon. "I know you have given your word to Edward that you will go, but promise me that you will make certain that your stepfather is also entertained."

"Yes, Mama," Lucia answered glumly, thinking that she might prefer to stay at home if she were forced to spend more than five minutes alone with her stepfather.

As they were discussing who else might be going to the ball, Sir Arthur walked into the bedroom.

"Are you feeling any better?" he asked without a hint of emotion in his voice.

"Yes, thank you, dear. I am just a little tired. I have asked Lucia to keep you company at the ball in a few days time."

Sir Arthur raised an eyebrow at his stepdaughter.

"I trust you are not thinking of rushing off to Bond Street to buy some over-priced gown or other. We must practice frugality in our current circumstances."

"I have a gown that will be most suitable for the occasion," responded Lucia bristling. "I am not the sort of girl who wears a dress once and then discards it."

"I am glad to hear it," he snapped. "I have been going over the household accounts and there are one or two economies I would wish to discuss with your mother. Now, leave us, Lucia."

Biting her lip to hold back her rising temper, Lucia squeezed her mother's hand and rose from the chair by the bedside.

'The manner in which he addresses me is so abrupt. I know that Northern folk have a reputation for plain speaking, but he is just plain rude.'

Later, at dinner, Lucia was relieved to see that her mother had made the effort to get out of bed and was making an attempt to eat some soup that cook had made for her.

"Are you feeling any better, Mama?" she asked kindly.

"A little, thank you, darling. I think the sleep did me some good."

Almost immediately she began to cough. At first, Lucia thought that perhaps some soup had gone down the wrong way, but she had already finished it.

"Mama!" she cried in alarm. "Perhaps we should call the doctor?"

"We cannot afford it unless your mother is very ill," cut in Sir Arthur without waiting for his wife to reply. "Doctors cost money and we do not have the brass to throw around at the moment."

"But if Mama needs it – "

"If I deem her ill enough to warrant the expense, then I shall call a doctor. Until then, we will look after her ourselves."

After summoning Moston to bring her a glass of water, her mother eventually recovered herself. With admirable composure, she resumed the conversation.

"Arthur, how did your meeting go today?"

"The accountants have advised me that it is not the right time to be selling Bingham Hall. War may be brewing in Europe and the property market is not good at the moment. There is no point in selling such a valuable asset for too low a price."

Lucia felt very relieved.

'At least I will not have to leave the County,' she thought.

"No, we shall have to think of another means to find twenty-five thousand pounds," continued her stepfather. "But there is not much time. I am attempting to secure the money, but we must not raise our hopes. I may have to resort to other avenues."

As he set down his glass, he threw Lucia a meaningful stare.

'Does this somehow involve me?' she thought with a sick feeling. 'The way he looked at me makes me believe he has some plan I am to be a part in.'

She knew that could mean only one thing – a suitable and profitable match.

Lucia finished her meal in silence. Although she had of late begun to think more about marriage, it would have to be under the right circumstances.

'Ideally, I would have to love and respect the man,' she thought, as she toyed with a plate of fruit. 'And I would need to find him attractive and handsome – "

Lucia was a little unworldly when it came to romance. Although she had found plenty of admirers in Paris, she had not taken them at all seriously.

Since she had returned to England, Edward de Redcliffe really was the only man who had even vaguely sparked her interest. And that was largely because he seemed so attracted to her and there was also the factor that Emmeline had seemed to be so keen to arrange a good match.

Lucia liked to please her friends and Emmeline was her oldest one. She had written numerous letters after that first meeting with Edward, asking Lucia when she might see him again and had he tried to kiss her yet?

Lucia felt as if Emmeline was willing something to happen between them in order to have the feather of their romance for her cap.

"*I have allowed him to call,*" she had written to Emmeline. "*He seems a solid and dependable soul, if a little old-fashioned. Mama likes him a great deal as she says he is well-mannered and respectful.*"

Not knowing any differently, Lucia told herself that she would be willing to settle for a man who was decent and upright like Edward. She knew that her stepfather, if he did indeed intend to try and make a match for her, would probably find someone a great deal older and set in his ways.

'Could I really marry someone to save Mama and Bingham Hall from ruin?' she asked her reflection, as Mary-Anne brushed her hair out later that evening. 'Papa always told me that I should put my family first and I suppose if I am forced to, I would do it, but only so that Mama would be looked-after and comfortable.'

Thanking Mary-Anne, she dismissed her and climbed into bed. She turned down the oil lamp by her bed and stared into the darkness of her room.

'Could I really marry a man I did not love and still be happy?' she mused. 'Perhaps Edward will propose and offer to help once he hears of our predicament. Maybe I should hope that he will ask me to marry him before stepfather finds another suitor for me. I should be so much happier if I felt as if I had some choice in the matter.'

With this thought comforting her, Lucia drifted off to sleep, trying to think of ways to make Edward fall in love with her.

*

The day of the ball soon dawned and, in spite of Lucia's attempts at persuasion, her mother could not be coaxed down from her bedroom.

"It will do you good to go out," she had said to her.

"No, dearest. I feel far too weak to stand up at a ball all evening. You go with Edward and your stepfather. Keep an eye on him and dance with him at least once – promise me?"

"Yes, Mama," agreed Lucia dutifully, feeling revulsion as she said the words.

She had not warmed to her stepfather any more since the day of the wedding and she felt as if she never would.

At the appointed time, Mary-Anne came to dress her. The lemon-silk dress flattered her complexion and made her eyes look bluer than their usual shade of grey. The dress was heavy with cream-coloured lace and she decided to wear her pearls to complement it.

"Will you be wearing your dancing slippers, miss?" asked Mary-Anne, opening the wardrobe.

"There are some cream ones at the back that I have not worn for a long while."

"You can't wear these, miss. Look, they are nearly threadbare in places."

Lucia sighed. She had quite forgotten that she had almost ruined them the last time she had worn them in Paris.

"Could you not freshen them up a little?" she asked hopefully.

Mary-Anne looked at them again.

"I'll see what I can do with a kettle and some steam," she replied. "I will be as quick as I can."

Half an hour later Mary-Anne brought them back.

"There," she beamed, bending down to slip Lucia's foot into one. "I won't say they're as good as new, but I've managed to patch up the holes. Just don't you go scuffing them together and they might hold. No one will be looking that closely at them, I'm sure."

Lucia wished she was quite as confident as her maid. She knew that every girl in the County would be present in her best clothes and that some took great pleasure in finding fault with each others' attire.

At that moment she heard the front door bell ring.

'That will be Edward,' she said to herself.

She rose, waited while Mary-Anne draped her white velvet coat with a fur collar around her shoulders and proceeded downstairs.

"Miss Lucia, Mr. de Redcliffe is in the drawing room," announced Moston.

"And my stepfather?"

"Briggs is bringing the Rolls Royce round to the front and he will follow you to the ball."

Lucia hesitated for a moment before entering the drawing room. Looking in the hall mirror, she pinched her cheeks and ran her tongue over her lips to make them dewy.

'There, I shall look my best.'

She knew by the way that Edward's eyes lit up when he saw her that she had achieved the desired effect.

"Lucia – how delightful you look," he said in his understated fashion.

He took her hand and kissed it.

"I noticed that your Rolls Royce is outside. I would prefer that we travelled in my carriage. I do not really care for motor cars."

"The Rolls Royce is waiting for my stepfather. He is also attending the ball this evening."

"Come," he said quietly, holding out his arm.

Lucia felt excited as they climbed into Edward's brougham. It was highly luxurious and she admired the fine interior.

"I hope it does not rain or your stepfather will find himself a trifle wet," Edward remarked, as a chilly wind blew through the open window.

"The Rolls Royce has a hood that comes over and protects one from the elements," answered Lucia.

"Nevertheless, you cannot make a comparison with the comfort that a good, old-fashioned carriage offers," he asserted, sliding the carriage window shut.

"Personally, I find driving a thrilling pastime," replied Lucia with a smile. "If you love the speed of horses, the motor car can provide just as much excitement."

"I doubt it," countered Edward with a confidence that

bordered on arrogance.

Lucia regarded him closely as the carriage pulled off down the drive. He was not unpleasing to the eye and he was intelligent.

'If only I did not suspect him of being a bit of an old fogey,' she thought, taking in the hazel eyes and neat, dark hair. 'But he is a good man of that I have no doubt.'

The ball was taking place in the magnificent surroundings of Thorley House, a Queen Anne building that had been in the Thorley family for many generations.

Carriages and one or two motor cars queued along the drive waiting to disburse their passengers.

Lucia looked to see if she could glimpse the Rolls Royce as Sir Arthur had overtaken them some miles back.

Soon their carriage was at the front of the queue and a liveried footman was opening the door. Edward helped Lucia down and up the steps to the house.

She noticed one or two people she knew and waited while another footman took their coats.

"Shall we go into the ballroom?" suggested Edward taking her arm again. "Or would you prefer to go to the Grand Hall?"

"I should love a glass of champagne," declared Lucia feeling full of excitement.

They had not gone more than a dozen paces when they met a group of friends.

"Emmeline," cried Lucia. "How beautiful you look."

"And your gown. I have not seen this one before, have I? Is it new?"

"It's from Paris," answered Lucia. "Look, there is Tristram and Cecily."

"Yes, I detect a whiff of romance there," gurgled Emmeline. "Shall we join them?"

As they moved towards the couple, Lucia reflected how much she would have hated to leave the County.

As she took a glass of champagne, she noticed her stepfather standing in the corner of the room conversing with someone. She smiled thinly at him and only barely registered the man who stood next to him. He was tall and dark-haired and she could not see his face as it was obscured by a woman standing in front of him.

'Another one of stepfather's business associates no doubt.'

After a while, the music began and Edward accompanied her into the ballroom. Lucia loved to dance and was most disappointed when Edward trod on her toes twice during a Viennese waltz.

'My slippers,' she thought anxiously. 'If he stands on my toes once more they will be utterly ruined.'

The dance ended and gratefully she allowed him to escort her from the floor.

"Really, Edward dances like a carthorse," whispered Emmeline, who had witnessed the whole affair.

"Oh, dear, here comes my stepfather. I shall have to dance with him, I suppose. I did promise Mama that I would look after him."

"He has been talking to that gentleman over there for a very long time. Is he a family friend?" asked Emmeline.

Lucia looked over and now saw the man to whom she was referring.

'A handsome man for his age,' thought Lucia fleetingly before answering, "I don't know who he is. I have not seen him at Bingham Hall."

"Ssh, here comes your stepfather."

Sir Arthur had taken some time to cross the ballroom as there were so many guests thronging the floor.

"Lucia," he said as he drew up beside her. "Would you care to dance?"

"Of course, Stepfather," she agreed, feeling unenthusiastic.

The orchestra had struck up a lively polka and Lucia almost winced at the first notes, fearing that her slippers would now be subjected to further damage.

However, to her surprise, he proved very light on his feet and, by the end of the dance, she had quite enjoyed herself.

"Who is the gentleman you were talking to?" she asked, as they danced.

"I am surprised that you have not met Lord Winterton," he replied. "He is a very important man in this County and owns Longridge Manor. It is about fifteen miles from Shilborough."

"How curious that we have not met," said Lucia. "I thought we knew most of the County families."

"I believe he spends a great deal of time in London these days and prior to that was in India. Lord Winterton is a very clever man and I admire his head for business. Since my arrival down South, he has often given me impeccable advice."

Lucia was a little surprised. Her stepfather had the air of a man who was full of self-confidence.

"Are we so very different, we Southerners?" she asked with a hint of sarcasm creeping into her voice.

"Southerners are fond of giving themselves airs and graces, whereas Northern folk take as they find. In Lord Winterton, I have found a man who, although aware of his position, does not seek to flaunt it in order to make a man feel small."

The dance ended and Lucia looked over to where Lord

Winterton now stood. There was something about those dark eyes that made her feel uneasy as they burned into her face and then travelled up and down her figure.

'He has an impudent manner,' she thought stiffly. 'I do not care to be gawped at as if I was a prize heifer at a cattle fair!'

She coolly returned his gaze and thought him one of those men who made a great deal of their masculinity in an almost uncouth way.

There was something about the tilt of his head as he stood in the shadows and the expression on his face. A sensual smile played about his mouth and his eyes were fiery beneath strikingly dark eyebrows.

Lucia forced herself to look away, but there was something about him that even now compelled her to search him out.

He made her feel uncomfortable and as if she should have worn something more modest.

'I despise men like him,' she said to herself, as she moved towards the Grand Hall in search of refreshment.

"Lucia." Edward called to her from his place by the French windows.

"Would you care for something to eat? The buffet is excellent."

"No, thank you. But I would like a glass of water – it is so hot in the ballroom."

"Who was that man with your stepfather?" asked Edward later, as he brought her a glass of water.

"Lord Winterton."

"I did not care for the way that he was staring at you as you danced with your stepfather. Had he persisted, I would have had words."

Lucia laughed.

"Oh, Edward, don't be silly! You were mistaken."

"I know when a man is staring in an uncouth manner and when he is not," answered Edward curtly.

He took Lucia's hand and held it for a few moments. She felt a little awkward, but allowed him the liberty.

After a while, she went to withdraw her hand, but he held onto her fast.

"Would you care to walk outside? I would very much like some fresh air."

Lucia nodded and put down her empty glass. A quick glance at her stepfather informed her that he was otherwise engaged and so she was happy to slip away from his scrutiny.

The moon was not yet full as they made their way along the path lit with Chinese lanterns hanging from graceful weeping beech trees.

"Come, there is a pond and fountain in the walled garden over there," whispered Edward. "I have heard that it is illuminated at night."

They walked under a pretty wrought iron arch and through a gate into a walled garden. Lucia gasped in wonder as they moved along the path as the fountain was lit with electric lights from inside the pond.

"Isn't it wonderful?" she murmured, admiring the effect of the water splashing out of the dolphin's spout in the middle of the fountain.

She turned to look at Edward and was stunned when he suddenly lunged forward and attempted to plant a kiss full on her mouth.

"*Edward*!" she cried moving to one side. "What are you doing?"

He leapt back as if he had been scalded.

"I'm sorry, Lucia. I did not mean to offend you. It was just that I was so intoxicated by the lights and your beauty."

Lucia pushed him firmly away and turned back towards the house.

"I think we should go inside," she said, hurrying back along the path.

"Lucia! Forgive me," called Edward, as he tried to catch up with her.

Back inside he found her by the buffet.

"Lucia, I am sorry – I – "

"Edward, we shall not mention it again."

"I thought you might not find the idea of kissing me repugnant."

"Indeed, I do not," she replied. "But there is a time and a place for that sort of thing. We must take things slowly."

"Of course, dearest. I am sorry. Say you'll come riding with me tomorrow otherwise I will not sleep tonight. I must know that I have not offended you so much that you will not continue to see me."

"Shall we ride out on your horses?" asked Lucia craftily. She harboured a desire to try out the fine chestnut stallion he had ridden to Bingham Hall when he came to call on her.

"Of course. My stables are at your disposal."

"Very well, I accept," she replied a little haughtily. She had remembered what her French friend, Janine, had said to her about treating gentlemen coolly as it only increased their ardour.

"Thank you. Thank you."

'It may be easier than I had believed to ensnare him,' thought Lucia, as they sought out a place to sit down.

She had barely taken a few mouthfuls of the prawn *vol au vents* when her stepfather came through the crowd towards her.

"Lucia, I would speak to you privately. I confess that I have tired of this ball and wish to return home. Are you ready to leave?"

Lucia looked at the clock. It was only half-past ten, but the incident with Edward had somewhat soured her evening.

"Let me finish these few morsels and I will come home with you," she agreed. "Edward, you will not mind if I leave now with my stepfather, will you?"

He hesitated for a moment and did not look at all pleased.

"Of course not," he answered, as etiquette demanded. "I will send my carriage for you tomorrow afternoon at two o'clock."

He took her hand and kissed it. As he moved away, he gave her a look that convinced her she had wounded him enough to make him want to come back.

"Goodnight, Lucia. Goodnight, Sir Arthur."

He turned round and was soon lost in the crowd.

"I will have the footman fetch your coat. I will wait for you at the entrance," said Sir Arthur dourly.

Lucia went to find Emmeline to bid her goodbye and then hurried out of the ballroom.

As she left, she caught a glimpse of Lord Winterton. He appeared deep in conversation with an attractive middle-aged woman who was wearing just a few too many diamonds.

His hot eyes followed her and she felt herself flush.

'He is so impudent,' she said to herself once again.

Sir Arthur was waiting for her along with a footman who held her velvet coat.

Briggs was already in the motor car with the engine running when they emerged into the chilly night air. The

46

hood had been pulled down and he pulled a warm woollen rug over her legs.

As the car drew away, her stepfather announced,

"Well, I have found a solution to our little problem."

Lucia felt sick.

'Why do I believe this might involve me?' she asked herself as her heart raced.

"I have struck a most agreeable deal with Lord Winterton," he continued. "He tells me that he finds himself lacking a good secretary and I happened to mention how good you are at replying to correspondence. Your Mama is forever praising your ability to write letters and so, when he said he required someone, I suggested *you*. In return for your services, he will lend me the money we need to get ourselves out of trouble."

Lucia was half elated and half horrified – she was not averse to the idea of working. After all, it would take her out of the house, but this was so sudden.

And the details of the deal were yet to be revealed. She assumed that she would be working for no remuneration in order to repay the debt.

"That is very generous of him," she answered slowly, "but I find it hard to believe that he will be happy with my working for him for nothing. I shall not accrue enough earnings in a million years, even if I work all day, every day"

Sir Arthur also took his time in replying. He did not meet her gaze, he simply continued to stare straight ahead as he answered her,

"You are a clever girl and I will not seek to pull the wool over your eyes. I have agreed to Lord Winterton marrying you after six months, should he find you agreeable."

Lucia felt as if the bottom had just fallen out of her world. She gripped on to the side of the car as it rocked around a corner and could hardly speak.

"You – have – bargained with me – as the security and deposit?" she stammered. "How could you do that? I do not wish to marry the man! Edward de Redcliffe – "

"Edward de Redcliffe is not offering me twenty-five thousand pounds to get us out of the trouble largely caused by your father's imprudence," he shouted flying into a rage. "I am now head of the house and, if you know what is good for you, you will do as I say without a word to the contrary!"

"But – "

"No more, Lucia. I have arranged for Lord Winterton to visit us tomorrow and you will receive him with a smile on your face. Is that clear?"

Lucia bowed her head trying to stem the tears welling up in her eyes. Perhaps if she had not been so hasty tonight in rebuffing Edward's advances, he might have proposed and then maybe he might have been able to help out.

But in her heart, she knew that, no matter how wealthy Edward might be, he did not have twenty-five thousand pounds at his disposal.

No, it was hopeless.

She felt so wretched as the motor car purred along the country lanes that she even considered jumping out.

'Right now, I would not care if I died,' she said to herself miserably. 'I cannot go and work for that man, there is something about him that is not – at all correct.'

But Lucia knew that she was helpless, utterly helpless. She was not in control of her own fate.

'Oh, Papa,' she wailed sending up a silent prayer to him in Heaven. 'Why did you have to die? Help me. Please, help me. I don't know if I can endure being treated like this.'

CHAPTER FOUR

Lucia's evening had been utterly ruined.

When the Rolls Royce arrived back at Bingham Hall, she ran straight inside without waiting for Sir Arthur and rushed at once to her bedroom.

She threw off her ruined slippers and pulled ferociously at her hairpins.

"Miss," cried Mary-Anne as she entered. She had not expected her back so soon. "Whatever is the matter?"

Lucia could not speak. She was so angry that she feared she might say something indiscreet and no matter how much she loathed her stepfather at that moment, it would not do to let the servants know.

"Help me get my dress off," was all she said looking forward to the moment when Mary-Anne would leave her on her own.

As soon as she had shut the bedroom door, Lucia threw herself onto the bed in a fit of rage.

'I cannot bear to think of having to work for that man,' she wept into her pillow.

Eventually exhaustion overtook her and, when she awoke the next morning, she was still lying on top of the coverlet.

Mary-Anne did not know whether she should remark

on her Mistress's state or not. She simply set down the tray with the early-morning cup of tea and went to run her bath.

The maid had only been out of the room for a matter of seconds when there came a knock on the door.

It was Mrs. Darrowby, the housekeeper, and it was only too apparent that she was upset.

"I'm sorry to disturb you so early, miss, but I thought I should come at once. Your Mama has taken a turn for the worse and I think we should call out the doctor."

"Does my stepfather know about this?" asked Lucia.

"I-I thought that perhaps you would speak to him about it."

Lucia sighed inwardly, but did not show her emotions.

"Very well, once I am dressed I shall go and see him. Is he at home this morning?"

"Yes, miss. He has already had his breakfast and is in the study."

A little later Lucia held her breath as she knocked on the door of the study.

"It is Mama. She is not at all well. Mrs. Darrowby has asked that we send for the doctor."

Sir Arthur exhaled and pursed his lips.

"She is gravely ill, sir," she said pleadingly. "I would not ask if it wasn't serious."

"You may summon Doctor Maybury from the village. I do not wish for my wife to suffer."

"Can I not call Doctor Glossop in Harley Street? He is far more experienced with chest complaints. He was wonderful with Mama when she was last ill – "

"Have you forgotten, Lucia, that we do not have Harley Street money? Until Lord Winterton has visited us this morning, the deal is not set in stone. No, Lucia, Doctor Maybury will suffice."

It was on Lucia's lips to retort that Doctor Maybury was a doddering old fool who could not cure a horse let alone a human, but she held her tongue.

"Thank you," she muttered quietly.

"And please wear something else to receive Lord Winterton this afternoon," called her stepfather as she turned to leave. "I trust you have not forgotten you have promised you would see him? I want you to make yourself as attractive as possible and that gown is far too cheap-looking."

Flushing scarlet Lucia closed the door behind her.

'How dare he?' she thought.

*

Her mother was not at all well. Her chest wheezed and her cough was now insistent. Mrs. Darrowby had propped her up in bed as, each time she lay back, she found it difficult not to cough.

When Lucia arrived, she found her mother with her face turned away and a worried-looking Mrs. Darrowby attempting to feed her.

She turned around and her dim eyes seemed to light up for a second.

"Lucia. Darling."

"Mama, the doctor will be calling this morning. I have just telephoned him."

"Doctor Glossop?" she asked eagerly.

"No, Mama. Doctor Maybury. He has said that he will be here as quickly as possible.

Upon hearing this news, she seemed to shrink. She had not cared for the man one bit when she had been ill the year before – he was a fool!

Lucia sat with her mother for a while and then she remembered that she had agreed to call on Edward that afternoon.

'I cannot go with Lord Winterton coming here,' she reasoned, rising from her chair and ringing for Mrs. Darrowby. 'I must telephone him at once.'

She asked Joyce at the Telephone Exchange to connect her to him. She felt certain that even though she did not have his number, it would not prove difficult to look up. After five minutes anxiously pacing the hall, the telephone rang.

"Your call to Mr. de Redcliffe, Miss Mountford."

"Hello, Edward?" she called into the mouthpiece.

"Lucia! What a wonderful surprise," he began. She could hear the eagerness in his voice.

"Edward, I am so sorry, but Mama is not at all well and I will not be able to come over to your house this afternoon. Would you mind terribly if we made it another time? I really want to look over your stables, but today is not the day."

There was a silence on the line as Lucia waited for his response. She gripped the telephone harder as she waited for him to speak.

"That's a pity," he said finally in a voice heavy with disappointment. "Please send her my best wishes for a speedy recovery. When would you like to come over?"

"We shall see, Edward. I have called out the doctor and much depends on his diagnosis. Perhaps I can telephone you again or write when I am able to visit?"

"Yes, of course. I am so sorry that your Mama is unwell. I will wait to hear from you."

"Goodbye, Edward."

Lucia felt heavy-hearted as she set the telephone back on the receiver.

She eyed her reflection in the mirror. She was wearing a white silk blouse that lit up her face and the pearls around her throat made her skin look soft and creamy.

'I feel as if I will be parading myself around as if I was for sale,' she thought. 'But then again, is that not precisely the case?'

Later that morning the doctor arrived and spent half an hour with her mother.

Lucia was called away before he left, as her stepfather wished to discuss some domestic matters with her.

By the time that the gong sounded for luncheon, Lucia's head was spinning with all the changes he wished to bring about at Bingham Hall. There were to be no more grand dinners, no May ball and, now that the motor car was used more than the carriages, Sir Arthur had mooted selling off some of the horses and the old phaeton.

Lucia wondered how everyone would receive the news. Theirs was one of the largest houses in that part of the County and the staff might find it difficult to find alternative employment.

He had also suggested laying off one or two other servants, until Lucia had explained that they were operating with the bare minimum for the size of the house.

As Moston served the soup, she felt pleased that she had been able to save their jobs. Moston had been with the family for many years and she did not know how the house would run without him.

"How is her Ladyship?" he asked as he spooned out the Mulligatawny soup.

"Sleeping," Lucia informed him. "Doctor Maybury gave her something to help her rest. I shall visit her once she is awake."

Lucia ate in silence. Her stepfather came and joined her, but they did not converse. He was as economical with his words as he was with his money. For once, she was completely at ease with that fact.

"I am glad you have decided to make yourself presentable," he commented as they left the dining room. "I am sure you will please Lord Winterton."

Lucia's stomach turned as he spoke and it was then she realised that she could not clearly recall Lord Winterton's face.

His lascivious expression – yes, but what colour eyes did he have? How old was he? She had assumed that he was her stepfather's age, but had not seen his face clearly.

'Well, I shall just have to wait and see,' she told herself, as she tried to pass the time.

On the dot of half-past two the front door bell rang. Lucia heard Moston go to answer it and then voices in the hall.

"The Master is waiting for you in his study," she heard him say.

After about fifteen minutes, Moston came to find her.

Lucia took a deep breath and felt as if she was walking to her doom. She smoothed back her hair and knocked on the study door.

The first person she saw as she entered was Lord Winterton and she was quite taken aback as he nodded in acknowledgment.

Far from being the older man she had thought she had seen, he was much younger, probably no more than thirty. He was also devastatingly handsome.

His striking blue eyes crinkled at the edges as he walked towards her.

"You did not meet my stepdaughter, Lucia, at the ball," intoned Sir Arthur.

Lord Winterton took her hand and kissed it. The shock of his moustache on her tender flesh sent shivers through her body.

"Charming," he said, releasing her hand. "Utterly charming."

His sensual mouth curved into a smile and, in spite of herself, Lucia felt her heart beating faster in response.

"I have spoken with her about becoming your secretary," began Sir Arthur. "And she is agreeable to the suggestion."

"You have a way with words or so I am told," interrupted Lord Winterton, his eyes raking up and down her frame. "I have need of a secretary with those kind of talents. Do you type?"

"I learned at Finishing School and achieved a distinction in the examination."

"Very impressive," he purred in a manner that hinted that he was not only referring to her secretarial abilities.

Lucia shrank beneath his penetrating gaze.

'That audacious stare,' she said to herself, trying not to appear too self-conscious. 'But he is so very handsome! Next to him, Edward is a mere boy.'

Lord Winterton moved with the grace of a panther. He walked across the room towards the windows exuding self-confidence and sensuality.

"I have an Underwood Number One – a truly marvellous piece of machinery. Do you think that you could master it?"

"I have already done so," replied Lucia with confidence. "That was the very machine that I used at school."

"Excellent," responded Lord Winterton, turning round to fix her with his gaze once more.

"I find that I need someone to reply to the many letters I receive," he continued. "I have several businesses both here and abroad and I need someone who is intelligent and can type. Sir Arthur, I would be glad to give your stepdaughter a trial as we discussed earlier. When would she be available?"

"As soon as you desire, Winterton," he replied with a satisfied smile. "Now, would you care for some refreshment?"

Lucia walked over to the bell and rang it. She noticed that Lord Winterton's eyes followed her as she moved across the room.

Moston came in with the tea ready made. He was excellent at anticipating his Master's needs.

Lord Winterton, who spoke amusingly about his time in India, largely dominated the conversation. By the time they had finished their tea, Lucia was in two minds what to think of him.

'He seems decent enough – but his manner,' she thought as she poured for their guest. 'He does not seem to care for the dictates of what is polite behaviour and what is not.'

After a while Sir Arthur spoke up,

"Lucia, would you leave Lord Winterton and me alone now? We have matters to discuss."

'*The marriage!*' she thought with a sick feeling.

Without protesting she rose and went to shake Lord Winterton's hand.

"I shall look forward to you coming to work at Longfield Manor," he said in his deep rich voice that seemed to strike a chord with something inside her.

Lucia felt herself blushing and hurried out of the room.

'What a perfect fool you are!' she said to herself crossly.

"Miss Lucia, this has just arrived for you."

Moston was coming towards her with a massive bouquet of exotic flowers in his arms. She knew who it was from before she even pulled out the card from between the heavy fragrant blooms.

"Thank you, Moston," she mumbled moving into the drawing room.

"*Wishing your mother a speedy recovery and that we see each other again soon, regards, Edward*," she read. 'Perhaps I should telephone him to thank him for them? I expect he meant them for Mama really.'

She rang for Moston and asked for the flowers to be taken up to her mother's room as soon as they had been arranged.

Lucia did not wish to appear too keen, so she waited until it late afternoon before she telephoned Edward.

"Thank you so much for the flowers. They will brighten Mama's room no end."

"I hope we can meet again soon," Edward insisted.

"As Mama is more stable, why don't you come over for a hack tomorrow?"

"I would love to and I shall bring Lightning so that you can ride him."

Lucia was thrilled.

"I should like that very much," she enthused with undisguised joy. "I have longed to ride him since the first day you brought him to Bingham Hall."

"Then it is settled, I shall see you tomorrow at say, ten o'clock?"

As Lucia replaced the receiver, she heard a noise behind her. Turning around, she came face-to-face with Lord Winterton.

"Oh, I had thought you had already left," she said colouring.

"I found that my discussion with your stepfather continued longer than I anticipated. I am glad to have the opportunity to say goodbye to you properly – you left so suddenly."

He smiled at her with a mischievous look on his face and once again, she felt quite uncomfortable under his scrutiny.

He stood towering over her. His broad shoulders filling out the lines of his overcoat to perfection and giving the impression of someone at once both in charge of himself and protective.

As he leaned in slightly towards her, Lucia found herself involuntarily taking a step backwards.

Lord Winterton silently acknowledged her retreat and straightened himself.

"I have made arrangements with your stepfather and will see you presently at Longfield Manor. He will discuss the details with you and I am afraid I have stayed far longer than I intended. Thank you for a charming afternoon. I found the company – most pleasing."

He bowed his head and took his hat from Moston.

"Good afternoon, Miss Mountford. I look forward to seeing you at Longfield Manor!"

He placed his hat on his head and then with one last lingering look walked out through the front door.

'Really!' said Lucia fanning herself. 'I can see that I shall have to watch him carefully when working for him. I would not put it past him to make unwelcome advances!'

While she had found it simple to rebuff the advances of flirtatious young Frenchmen, Lord Winterton was a fully grown man of considerable personal magnetism and not a gauche but charming boy.

'I do hope there will not be any unnecessary unpleasantness,' she thought, feeling a little afraid, as she watched Moston close the front door.

Lucia silently mounted the stairs to her mother's room. She pushed the door open just a crack and looked inside. The room was in semi-darkness and both Mrs. Darrowby and her mother were fast asleep.

She smiled and closed the door softly.

'Perhaps Mama will be right as rain in a few days,' she mused returning back downstairs.

As she reached the foot of the stairs, her stepfather intercepted her.

"Lucia, come to the study, would you?"

She followed him into the room and was surprised to find that there lingered on the air an odour that reminded her of Lord Winterton. Was it cologne, she wondered, or cigars mingled with leather? She could not make up her mind.

In any event it unnerved her and made her feel as if he was still in the room.

"I am pleased that Lord Winterton found you to his liking," he began, refusing to meet her gaze. "He has indicated that he wishes you to start at once."

"But Mama – "

"She would not wish to stand in the way. She would understand that such matters are not her business and now you will make ready to leave the Hall early on Monday morning. Lord Winterton will require you to stay at Longfield Manor during the week and you will be allowed home at weekends."

'Live in,' thought Lucia shocked, 'but that is something servants do.'

"But it is not so far that I could not travel each day and Mama needs me. She is far from well and I would never forgive myself should anything happen to her."

Sir Arthur whirled around from his position by the

window with his eyes bulging with fury.

"Lucia, this is not the first time I have had to tell you that what I say goes. You will do as you are told and without complaint. Heavens! How many times must I say this? You will start on Monday. Please arrange for your bags to be packed and Briggs will take you straight after breakfast. Now let that be the last of this nonsense. Your Mama will be perfectly cared for by Mrs. Darrowby."

Lucia ran from the room to hide the fact that she was starting to cry.

'I must not show him how upset I am,' she determined, as she returned upstairs. 'But I am just a pawn in my stepfather's game of chess.'

She was just about to make for her room when she saw Mrs. Darrowby coming towards her with an anxious look on her face.

"Oh, Miss Lucia. There you are. I've been looking for you."

"Mama – she is not worse?"

"No, she is still sleeping, but I would speak with you in private."

Lucia led her into her room and closed the door.

"What is it, Mrs. Darrowby?"

"If I may speak plainly, miss. It's Doctor Maybury. I don't think he is very good. He barely examined the Mistress this morning and then proclaimed that she was suffering from a slight chest infection."

"Mama has had this trouble before."

"No, miss. I knows chest infections. She was bringing up blood before the doctor came and I did not like to alarm you. He did not seem interested when I told him, but who am I to argue with such a man?"

Lucia thought for a while before replying. Her

stepfather would not countenance her sending for Doctor Glossop and she had no money to speak of herself.

"Mrs. Darrowby, we must do our best with what resources we have. Watch Mama like a hawk and if there is any change, you must send for me."

"Send for you? Why, are you going away?"

"From Monday, I will be away from the house during the week, but I shall return home at weekends. You will have to manage."

Mrs. Darrowby's face crumpled.

"Oh!" she cried. "I don't know how the Mistress will take this news. Is this your stepfather's doing?"

"Hush. There is nothing to be gained by apportioning blame. I do not wish to alarm you, Mrs. Darrowby, but we find ourselves in difficult circumstances. I would ask you to bear whatever hardship comes along until such time as things improve."

"Of course, miss," she sniffled in response. "I'll go and make some tea."

Mrs. Darrowby left the room and Lucia dissolved into tears.

'She is right. How will Mama bear the news that I am to be sent away all week? It should be my stepfather who breaks it to her – not me or a servant.'

She hit the pillows in anguish.

'I would never forgive myself if this contributed to Mama's demise,' she sobbed. 'And I would never, never speak to my stepfather again either.'

But she knew that her fate was sealed and that her future lay some ten miles away at Longfield Manor.

CHAPTER FIVE

Lucia wandered over to her mother's room. Quietly she opened the door and put her head inside. Her mother was asleep and her mouth had fallen slightly open. Her skin was grey and her breathing laboured.

It brought tears to Lucia's eyes to see her.

'Mama ' she cried under her breath.

Tiptoeing quietly towards the bed, Lucia smoothed down the coverlet and sank down in the chair close by.

She sat there for a while gazing at her mother while her heart contracted with sorrow.

'What will I do if we lose her? She looks so ill.'

Lucia looked at the cluster of bottles on the bedside cabinet and picked up each one in turn.

Taking up the brown bottle at the back with a cork stopper, she furrowed her brow at the dried trickle of fluid that had collected around the rim.

'I shall speak with Mrs. Darrowby about ensuring better hygiene in the sick room,' she muttered to herself.

It was then that she noticed the printed label.

'*Laudanum*!' she gasped in horror.

At the same moment, Mrs. Darrowby came into the room with the tea tray.

"There you are, miss. I went to your room and found

the door wide open. I thought I'd find you here."

"Mrs. Darrowby, are you aware that Doctor Maybury had prescribed laudanum to Mama?"

She cast down her eyes and looked uneasy.

"I told the doctor that you would not be happy, but he told me to mind my own business and be sure not to give her any of my, what he called, *witches potions.*

"I would rather you had given her something of your own making, Mrs. Darrowby. You should have brought this to my attention."

"I am sorry, miss. I was going to and then I became distracted."

Lucia sighed and handed the bottle to Mrs. Darrowby.

"Please put this concoction down the sink at once. I do not mean to chastise you, but I will not have my Mama taking that filthy stuff!"

Mrs. Darrowby went into the bathroom and threw the liquid down the plug. Upon returning, she quickly poured some tea and handed a cup to Lucia.

"Lucia, is that you?"

Her mother opened her eyes and seemed distressed.

"Mama, I am here," said Lucia soothingly. "Now you must rest and not exert yourself."

"Where is your stepfather?" she asked. "He has not been in to see me today."

"He is occupied with business matters, Mama. How are you feeling?"

"A little woozy. The medicine that doctor gave me has such a bitter flavour."

"Mama, I need to speak with you."

"Is something wrong, darling?" asked her mother looking dismayed.

"Nothing to alarm yourself about. It is just that I shall not be at the Hall during the week for the foreseeable future. Stepfather has found me employment."

"Employment!" she cried, trying to sit up in bed. "What nonsense is this?"

"Mama, I have no choice. Lord Winterton has kindly offered to help us out of our current financial plight and in return, I will work for him as a secretary."

A low moan came from her mother.

"Oh, is this what we are reduced to? My daughter forced to take work as a mere secretary."

"But I shall not be just a secretary, Mama. Besides, I cannot withdraw as my working for him is a condition of the loan. Lord Winterton is an important man in the County and from what he says, he needs help in running his many businesses."

"He means he needs help escaping from his paramours. Oh, Lucia! He is not the kind of man you should be working for. *The man is a rake!*"

Lucia was shocked at her mother's vehemence. Her eyes were staring and she seemed to be very distressed.

"He has led a life of looseness and has dubious morals," she continued. "No woman is safe in his presence. I hope he has arranged a chaperone for you? If not, you must insist. You cannot have your reputation ruined and you know I have long desired that you make a good match when the time comes for you to be married."

A lump rose in Lucia's throat.

'How can I tell Mama that I am part of the bargain?' she thought as she watched her mother begin to cry.

"I am certain that he is not as black as he is painted, Mama – " she began.

"You do not know him. You are young and innocent

and not familiar with the ways of men such as he. He is a marriage wrecker and thinks nothing of compromising the virtue of ladies. Why, only last year, some poor wretch had to be sent away to the coast."

Lucia grasped her mother's meaning at once. There was only reason why young ladies from good families were sent away.

Her mother continued her diatribe without pausing.

"And then, there was that Lady Shelley. Such a shocking affair!"

"Lady Shelley?" asked Lucia, not following the thread of the conversation.

"Yes. I know I should not listen to gossip, but then I saw them together with my own eyes, making a spectacle of themselves at Ascot. Your father forbade me to speak to either of them after that. Poor Lord Shelley, the old fool did not realise what was going on right under his nose. Of course, he has now passed away."

"Mama. You must not upset yourself. I am quite capable of taking care of myself. Look, here is Mrs. Darrowby."

Lucia was grateful of the chance to steer the conversation away from the topic of Lord Winterton. Had not her mother just confirmed all her worst fears about him?

"I shall leave you now, Mama, but I shall look in again before dinner."

Closing the door behind her, Lucia returned to her room. Lord Winterton's arch face suddenly flashed into her mind and she willed it away.

'What is it about that man that makes him so – impertinent?' she asked.

'I shall resolve to keep my distance and Mama is right, I should request a chaperone. Yes, I shall insist on it!'

*

The next day, Lucia made herself ready to receive Edward. She had not forgotten that she had invited him with his stallion to the Hall for a ride.

She did her best to avoid discussing anything over and beyond the marmalade at breakfast with her stepfather.

As soon as she had finished eating, she left the dining room and went out to the stables to check that everything was ready.

"Will you be riding Flash today, miss?" asked Jack.

"No, but Mr. de Redcliffe will," she replied. "Have him saddled up, please."

She watched Jack walk away and wondered if he had any inkling that the future of the stables had been in serious jeopardy.

Now with Lord Winterton's promise of funds, they would not be selling horses.

"Lucia."

She turned around in time to see Edward riding towards her on Lightning. The horse tossed his dark mane and snorted as he pulled up next to her.

"Good morning, Edward. I see that Lightning is in fine form today."

"He is being rather skittish actually, I do hope that he behaves for you."

"I am told that I ride as well as any man and I love a challenge. I have selected Flash for you to ride. He is a very handsome stallion with a fondness for eating daisies!"

"Then it is fortunate that the daisies are not yet out," remarked Edward.

Lucia stroked Lightning's fine, well-muscled neck and spoke to him gently.

"There, my fine boy. We shall have some fun today."

Very soon she was astride him and they were heading along the fields at the back of Bingham Hall.

Lucia could not resist the temptation to show off a little and made Lightning take a jump over a hedge at the edge of the estate. The horse flew through the air and landed sure-footedly on the other side.

Lucia felt as if she had grown wings.

After a long hard ride, they came to a halt by a stream. There they allowed the horses to drink.

"You had me worried for a moment when you went for that hedge," admitted Edward, as they sat down on a fallen tree trunk. "It was rather daffy of you."

"Not at all," replied Lucia confidently. "I have been riding horses since I could walk. I know what I am doing with them."

"Even so, Lightning is a very spirited blighter."

"He is, but he is not uncontrollable."

They fell into a companionable silence. And then, without warning, Edward seized Lucia's bare hand and covered it with kisses.

"Edward," she cried, trying to pull it away.

"Lucia, will you marry me?" he demanded hoarsely. His eyes were burning into her, entreating her to reply affirmatively.

"Edward, what madness has overtaken you?"

She scrabbled in the grass for her discarded gloves with her free hand.

"It's not madness. You must know that I love you desperately. I intend to speak with your stepfather this very day!"

"No, you must not!" cried Lucia, rising and extricating her hand from his.

"Why ever not?"

'If I say I am already promised, he will tell his friends and everyone will gossip,' she thought hurriedly, searching for an excuse that would satisfy him.

"It – it is not the right time," she murmured.

Edward's face suddenly came to life.

"Your Mama, of course, how insensitive of me. I am sorry, but I have quite forgotten myself."

"We should return home," said Lucia, as they awkwardly faced each other.

"I will wait for you," pleaded Edward. "Please do not refuse me."

"I will see," answered Lucia, untethering Lightning's reins.

Edward looked relieved.

"Thank you," he breathed coming closer. "Will you seal it with a kiss?"

"*No, I shall not,*" replied Lucia haughtily, as she pulled herself up onto Lightning's back. "We must return to the Hall without further delay. My stepfather will be wondering where I am."

Digging her heels into Lightning's side, she shot off, leaving Edward gazing impotently after her.

*

The mood was rather subdued on their return.

Edward took his leave, asking that she think about his proposal and then promised to call on her the following weekend.

As he left Sir Arthur pulled up in the Rolls Royce.

"I hope you are not encouraging him," he said as he watched Edward ride off. "You will give yourself a bad reputation and Lord Winterton will not like it."

Lucia refrained from saying that, according to her

mother, Lord Winterton did not have any room to be taking any kind of high moral ground.

Sir Arthur continued to remind her of her duty throughout the rest of the weekend. He constantly picked her up on her attitude and by Sunday evening she was almost looking forward to leaving so that she did not have to endure him any longer.

'If only Mama was not so ill,' she thought. 'I would not mind leaving her. The way my stepfather speaks to me is outrageous and he is not even my real father!'

She picked up the photograph of Lord Mountford from her dressing table and looked at it for a very long while.

"Please put this in my hand luggage and wrap it up in a silk scarf to protect it, Mary-Anne," she said, handing her the photograph.

She looked around to search for one of her mother and spied a small silver-frame on her chest of drawers.

"And this one as well, please," she added.

'It's one of my favourites,' she told herself with a smile. 'Mama must have been my age when it was taken and she had just announced her engagement.'

Once again, Lucia's thoughts turned to marriage.

'I never imagined that I would be sold off in exchange for a house. I think Mrs. Pankhurst and her Suffragettes still have much work to do before we are considered anything other than men's chattels.'

Although not entirely sympathetic to their cause, Lucia took a keen interest in the exploits of Mrs. Pankhurst and her daughters.

'But, women getting the vote? I cannot see men allowing us such power.'

As Mary-Anne fastened the last trunk, Lucia found herself wondering more about Lord Winterton.

'Why is he not married already? I don't understand it. Although he is not quite as old as I had first believed – he is in the prime of his life and it is surprising he does not have a wife.'

But she knew that there were men like him, those who favoured the single life as opposed to the comfort and security of marriage.

'Perhaps he has just not found the right woman. That Lady Shelley does not sound a suitable wife at all. Although I can imagine that she would set her cap at him, especially as she is now a free agent.'

She was still pondering the conundrum when she climbed into bed that night.

'I should stop thinking about him as it's not healthy to have such an interest in him,' she scolded herself. 'He is to be my employer and his private affairs will be none of my concern.'

But there was something about Lord Winterton that kept him on her mind long into the night.

*

All too soon Lucia found herself in the Rolls Royce on her way to Longfield Manor.

The drive there was considerably quicker than by carriage and it seemed as if they had only been travelling for a short while before the motor car slowed down in front of the ornate iron gates, beyond which lay Longfield Manor.

'Here, already,' she sighed, as Briggs went to open the gates.

She had not been to the Manor before and, under happier circumstances, would have enjoyed a visit. But now she felt only sick to her stomach with nerves.

'Lord Winterton has a great deal of land,' she murmured, as they passed a wood, a lake, fields full of sheep and a large paddock where several horses ran free.

'I hope he will allow me to ride in my free time,' she mused, eyeing a particularly beautiful dapple-grey mare that trotted along the perimeter fence.

Briggs manoeuvred the Rolls Royce along the gravel drive and came to a halt outside the heavy double doors that served as a front entrance.

Almost as soon as he had switched off the engine, a liveried footman appeared followed by a young boy also in livery.

Lucia stepped on to the gravel and looked up at the gables and orange bricks.

"Those latticed windows seem very old," she said out loud.

"Yes, they are, sixteenth century actually."

Lucia turned her head to see Lord Winterton striding towards her.

'He is not wearing a jacket,' she thought, shocked at his informality.

His shirt was open at the neck and, as he walked, it flapped open to reveal a muscular chest, thick with brown hair. Blushing, Lucia averted her eyes.

'Really!' she said to herself.

Although she could not deny that the sight of such obvious masculinity affected her in a manner that she could not quite quantify.

"Welcome to Longfield Manor," continued Lord Winterton. "It's a very old building and rather eccentric, but I am very fond of it. Wintertons have lived here since 1623 and my great-grandfather made many alterations in the name of modernisation. I intend to embark upon a series of improvements myself one day. But somehow, I never seem to find the time."

He aimed his hot gaze directly at Lucia's face and once again she found herself blushing uncontrollably.

'If only he did not make me feel so awkward,' she thought, as he escorted her into the elegant hall with its heavy oak staircase and floor-to-ceiling panelling.

In spite of herself, she felt strangely drawn to him. It was as if a spell was cast and she was helpless in its thrall.

As they walked along, she could feel the heat emanating from him.

He moved with a vulpine grace and she could not help but stare at his fine shape as he walked in front of her.

His shoulders were broad and strong and his muscular torso tapered to a narrow waist with an elegance that became him. She tried not to notice the strong legs as he strode purposefully towards a room at the end of a long gallery. It was filled with portraits in oils and Lucia assumed they were of his ancestors.

"I hope you will not mind if you begin at once. It is just that I have an appointment in a while and I am a little late."

He turned towards her as he opened the door and flashed a smile that touched something inside of her.

"Come and see my Underwood Number One," he called, obviously proud of the fact that he owned a typewriting machine.

Inside the study was a desk with the typewriter all ready for use, a letter rack holding sheets of crested notepaper and a stack of letters yet to be opened.

"You will sit there," he said, gesturing towards the desk. "If the chair is not comfortable, you must tell me at once and I shall have Jepson arrange for another to be brought in. I want you to feel at home," he added in a low confidential tone.

Lucia did not dare to stand too close to him. There was something overwhelmingly manly about him that unnerved her.

'Compared with him, Edward is a wet youth,' thought Lucia, as Lord Winterton ran through the names of the servants and what they did.

He seemed quite unabashed that when he leaned forward over the desk to show her something, his shirt fell open and exposed his abundantly hairy chest.

'Is he attempting to seduce me by showing off his body in this way?' she asked herself, as she inched away from him.

"Mama has asked that I have a chaperone," she said suddenly.

"Really?" answered Lord Winterton arching one elegant eyebrow. He stroked his moustache. "You don't wish to compromise your reputation?"

Lord Winterton laughed softly and then smiled to himself.

"In that case, I shall ask my housekeeper to keep you company or I am certain Antoinette, whom you shall meet later, would be happy to sit with you. I would have thought that in the circumstances you would not have required a nanny – "

He stared at her and Lucia felt a surge of anger.

'Is he intimating that I am immature and unable to look after myself?' she thought. 'How dare he!'

It had also not escaped her notice that he had made an oblique reference to the fact that they were unofficially betrothed. She was so cross that she could not reply.

"Now," he continued, without waiting for an answer, "answer those letters and I will return shortly. I have business to attend to. Are there any other questions?"

"No," replied Lucia still smarting from his previous comment. "I am sure I will manage."

She sat down in the leather chair and ran her fingers over the keyboard of the typewriter. In an instant she was transported back to her Parisian Finishing School.

Lord Winterton stood in the doorway of the study and gave a quick smile before disappearing.

Immediately, Lucia let out a sigh of relief and set about familiarising herself with her desk.

'Fountain pen, pencils, ruler, eraser,' she ticked off. 'Typing paper, notepad, letter opener. Yes, it all appears to be here.'

She stared at the pile of letters. Some of them had been opened, but others were still sealed.

"Surely he cannot mean me to open them before he has seen them?" she wondered out loud.

At the same moment, Jepson, the butler, came into the room.

"I could not help but overhear, Miss Mountford. I think you will find that his Lordship does indeed wish you to open everything. You will find that he is unusually observant and only opens the correspondence he knows he will wish to read. The others, ahem, you may wish to discard."

"Surely not? At least I should open them and draft a reply for Lord Winterton?"

"As you wish, Miss Mountford. You will find that he has made notes on the letters that he has read to guide you in your choice of response. Now, may I bring you tea or coffee?"

Lucia requested tea and then began to tackle the pile of letters.

The first one was an invitation to dinner at Claridge's with the Duke and Duchess of Argyll. *"Yes, would be delighted*," it read in a strong pencilled script.

'He has a very manly hand,' thought Lucia, as she opened a letter from a wine merchant, informing Lord Winterton of the arrival of a new shipment.

Having read all the opened letters, Lucia set about replying to them. Before she knew it, she had reduced the pile considerably.

"There. That did not take long,' she murmured, as she wrote all his new engagements into the desk diary she had found on the desk. 'Now, should I open these as Jepson suggested?'

She picked up the first unopened letter and regarded it carefully. The postmark was London and the hand a fine one.

'From a lady?' she thought and then decided that someone's secretary had most likely addressed it.

Pulling out the creamy paper she could see that it was covered in handwriting.

"My dearest Richard," she read. *"How cruel of you to leave so early last evening."*

Lucia coloured and quickly put the letter back into its envelope. She had not seen the signature and she did not want to, in case she knew the lady in question.

'Well,' she said to herself. 'Maybe Mama was right, but how odd that he has not opened it and left it on the pile with his business correspondence. It must be a mistake. Oh dear, I shall have to own up to him that I accidentally opened something private. I do hope he will not be cross with me.'

She quickly flicked through the remainder of the unopened letters and guessing that most of them were also from ladies, she set them to one side.

Before she knew it the gong had sounded for luncheon. She stretched and rose from her chair, wondering where she would find the dining room.

Fortunately Jepson was in the hall waiting for her.

"Do come this way, Miss Mountford. His Lordship is just upstairs and he will join you shortly."

She followed Jepson into the dining room. It was a large room with a huge crystal chandelier that hung over an imposing mahogany table.

There were flowers on the table and she noticed that the water glass in front of her was of the best crystal.

'He must be very rich,' she mused. 'We would not bring out such glasses for luncheon.'

"Good afternoon."

Lord Winterton's deep voice resonated around the large room.

He was wearing a dark-blue lounge coat and one of the latest shirts with a fashionably modern collar. His coat made his eyes look even bluer and more startling than ever. Lucia was forced to admit that he was indeed an extremely handsome man.

"I trust that you found your first morning passed swiftly and usefully?"

"Yes, sir," she answered, "I have finished replying to all your opened letters. I have to confess that I opened a letter from a lady by mistake. I hope you will forgive me for the intrusion into your privacy."

To her amazement Lord Winterton threw back his head and laughed throatily.

"My dear, I put those unopened letters in the pile so that you might reply on my behalf. They are from silly women whose heads are full of fanciful notions about the true nature of our involvements. I reasoned that you would be able to put them off with one of your clever replies."

Lucia did not know how to respond.

"Well – " she began.

"Oh, just thank them for taking the time to write and that their comments have been noted. Something like that. Sign it on behalf of me – a personal signature would only enflame them further."

"If you are certain."

"Dashed certain, my dear Lucia," he replied, buttering his roll generously. "Now, what's for luncheon, Jepson? I am famished."

Lord Winterton's Chef had excelled himself. Lucia had not tasted such delicious soup for ages and the lamb chops were superb.

"I must congratulate you on your Chef. A very fine meal."

"Old Francois is very talented," remarked Lord Winterton, finishing his glass of claret. "I found him in Paris when I was staying there a few years ago. Dashed glad I persuaded him to come and work for me."

"I attended Finishing School in Paris," said Lucia, pleased to have a topic of conversation she could speak about with authority.

"Really? Don't tell me you were one of those gels with the straw boaters? I always thought they looked rather fetching."

"Yes, we had to wear straw boaters, but only in the summer."

"Where did you attend?"

"It was the Lycée International not far from the Champs Elysees."

"Ah, I do not know it. My hotel was in Opera. And then I stayed with the Comtesse for a while – "

He tailed off, obviously recollecting a pleasant memory as he gazed into the middle distance and the expression on his face was one of rapt delight.

"Enough of that. Shall I ask Jepson to bring in the pudding? I think you will enjoy what I have chosen for you."

He nodded at Jepson and at the same moment the front door bell rang.

"Shall I answer the door first, my Lord?" asked Jepson.

"If you must," replied Lord Winterton wearily loosening his tie. "Tell them I am not at home, whoever it is."

"Very good, my Lord."

Jepson left the room and Lucia toyed with her glass of water. Lord Winterton had returned to his Parisian reverie and did not speak.

A few moments later, Jepson reappeared in the dining room.

"My Lord, you have a visitor."

"I thought I said I was not at home, Jepson?"

He sighed with irritation and threw his napkin impatiently down on the table.

"Begging your pardon, my Lord. I think you may wish to see this particular visitor."

Lord Winterton raised an eyebrow and huffed again. In a flash, Lucia realised that the visitor was most likely female.

"Very well. Take my visitor into the drawing room."

He was just in the process of rising when the door flew open and there, in a hat that defied gravity with its numerous ostrich plumes and a fur wrap with more paws than were plausible, was a woman. And a very beautiful woman at that.

"Run along, Jepson," she said huskily. "Shoo!"

She entered the room in a cloud of French perfume

that Lucia recognised as being extremely expensive.

The woman turned her brilliant violet eyes upon Lucia and looked her up and down. There was more than a hint of a sneer on her lovely face as she examined her in great detail.

"Richard," she purred. "Have you cast me aside already in favour of this – "

She gestured urgently at Lucia with one gloved hand. A large emerald bracelet slid down her arm and rattled as she pointed. Her face wore a petulant expression and she curled her lip in thinly disguised disgust.

"Who is this, Richard?" she demanded imperiously.

Lord Winterton let out a long sigh of resignation. He did not even look at the woman who now stood in the middle of the room in a pose that bristled with fury.

He plucked at his discarded napkin and slowly raised his eyes to meet Lucia's.

The woman was now leaning forward and Lucia wondered if she was about to attempt to strike her. Everything about her spoke of anger and violence.

Finally Lord Winterton spoke,

"Miss Mountford, this is Lady Shelley," he said without a vestige of embarrassment.

"Camilla, this is Miss Lucia Mountford."

Lucia sat tensely and watched as the woman began to move forward.

'What is she going to do? Oh, goodness! I do wish I wasn't here.'

CHAPTER SIX

Lady Shelley regarded Lucia with same kind of dismissive air as she might an inferior person. Her lovely mouth curled and she almost spat out her next sentence.

"Is this another of your playthings, Richard?" she snarled with a venomous tone in her voice. "I must say – this one is young, even by your standards."

Lucia felt most affronted by this insult and began to rise from her seat as a jolt of anger surged through her.

"I am not a child. I am twenty-one and have been engaged as Lord Winterton's new secretary," she snapped, leaping to her own defence.

"A likely story!" retorted Lady Shelley, eyes staring dangerously.

Lord Winterton simply fingered his moustache and seemed to be thoroughly enjoying both women's discomfiture.

"Camilla, you are wrong as usual," he intervened eventually, as the two women glared at each other.

"This young lady is who she says she is. As I am spending so much time in London, matters here are becoming unmanageable. I needed a secretary and Miss Mountford is the daughter of a friend of mine. Now, come, let us withdraw to the library. I have some new etchings I wish to show you."

Lady Shelley seemed to visibly retreat from her provocative stance and his assurances appeared to mollify her.

Lord Winterton rose from the table and then, as he passed her, he slapped her on the behind in a gesture that Lucia found both shocking and overly familiar.

'Well,' she said to herself, as the pair left the room. 'And she did not even apologise to me. What a rude woman!'

She waited while Jepson served coffee and did not dare to leave the dining room for fear of another unpleasant encounter with the imperious Lady Shelley.

'Perhaps Mama was not raving as I had supposed. Have I not just seen with my own eyes what sort of man he is? And it is plain as day what sort of woman Lady Shelley might be!'

Just then the unmistakable sound of giggling could be heard from the library next door. Jepson feigned a lack of hearing, but Lucia failed to see how he could not have been aware of the obvious activity.

"More coffee, Miss Mountford?" he asked, as she cast down her eyes and tried not to take notice of the numerous sounds that were coming from the library.

Lucia finished her coffee quickly and then returned to the study.

As she walked along the corridor, she bumped into a footman who was heading for the library with a silver tray, two glasses and a bottle of champagne.

'Well! Champagne in the afternoon,' she thought to herself.

But she could not help but feel the tiniest hint of jealousy that no one had ever brought champagne for her at such a scandalous hour.

She could not for one moment imagine the stiff and proper Edward even entertaining the notion.

'Ah, Edward – " she remembered as she returned to the study. She supposed herself to be rather fond of him. How could she not like a man who was as fine a horseman as he was? – but his ardour had unnerved her.

Her attention was soon distracted by the sounds of yet more laughter.

'I wish they would be quiet,' she thought, crossly, as she worked on.

Almost at once, there came an audible sigh and then silence.

With her ears straining, Lucia waited for a few moments, heard no more and continued typing.

But halfway through a letter, she found she had made too many mistakes.

'Oh, Heavens. I am more out of practice than I had imagined.'

She took the letter out of the machine and looked for a fresh sheet of paper, but she could not find a single piece anywhere on the desk.

'Perhaps there is some in the desk drawers?' she pondered, pulling one open.

There were a few envelopes and pencils inside and she could not help but notice a cheque book. Knowing that she should not, she slid it out of the drawer slowly and opened it.

Almost the first stub she came across was one clearly marked *Sir Arthur McAllister* and had been made out for the sum of twenty-five thousand pounds.

'So, the bargain has been sealed,' she muttered, putting it quickly back into the drawer.

Every now and then she would pause in her work and listen out for signs of life in the room next door, but it was ominously silent. She only wished it was not quite so obvious what was going on.

'Come and see my etchings indeed!' she snorted. 'I wonder if my stepfather knows that I am working for a man with loose morals and thinks nothing of flaunting his amours in front of his servants and his secretary?'

Her own father, she knew, would no sooner have compromised the reputation of his daughter than he would have eaten dinner with the wrong set of cutlery.

'Oh, Papa,' she prayed, momentarily forgetting the duties at hand. 'I hope that you are watching over Mama and willing her better. I miss you so very much.'

It was all she could do not to cry as her eyes threatened to fill with tears. Quickly, she searched for something else to do and noticing another pile of letters she began to inspect them.

Sure enough they were yet to be answered, each one with pencilled notes from Lord Winterton, guiding her as to how to respond.

And again there were unopened letters that she supposed to be from ladies.

She stood with the silver letter opener poised over the first one, hesitant.

'Well, he did say I should open everything and compose a clever reply,' she exclaimed before slitting it open.

She quickly scanned the contents. It was in the same vein as the other letter. Another lady, this time a Mrs. Radford-Hall, had written entreating him to visit her the following weekend as her husband was away in Scotland.

'Does Lady Shelley know that she is not the only woman in his life?' she wondered, as she quickly composed a suitably efficient yet noncommittal reply.

It occurred to her that Lord Winterton may have been playing a game with her.

'Perhaps he seeks to shock and finds sport in outraging me,' she debated. 'Well, I will prove to him that I am not easily ruffled!'

With the letter to Mrs. Radford-Hall completed, she opened another and another.

She replied to a rather important Duchess, a French Comtesse and a woman who simply signed herself, *your own Margaretta*.

As she put the finishing touches to the last one, she heard Lady Shelley's voice outside in the hall. Then the front door opened and closed.

"Thank Heavens she has gone," said Lucia out loud.

Not five minutes later, a rather dishevelled-looking Lord Winterton appeared in the study. He seemed quite unabashed about the fact that his waistcoat was partially undone and his hair was no longer neat and tidy.

"Ah, Lucia. I have a rather urgent missive from my Solicitor that I would ask you to reply to. It came a few hours ago. Are you able to take dictation?"

"Of course, I excelled in stenography," replied Lucia taking up pencil and pad.

Lord Winterton fiddled with his waistcoat buttons as he dictated the letter. It appeared that he was in the process of buying some land at the edge of his estate.

Lucia bowed her head and tried not to stare as his powerful fingers caressed the buttons – the same fingers that had no doubt just caressed Lady Shelley's face.

The image of him trailing his hands against Lady Shelley's white throat would not leave Lucia's mind and she was shocked at herself. And even more she actively wondered what it might feel like to have him caress her own skin in such a way.

'It is his bad influence in this bad house that is causing me to have such thoughts,' she said to herself, as he walked around the room, pausing to think of his next sentence.

At five o'clock on the dot, Lord Winterton lost all interest in dictation and announced that the working day was now over.

"I will ring for Jepson and ask him to show you upstairs. I am certain that you are eager to see your room. Now, if you will excuse me, I shall see you at dinner. Do not worry – we shall not be interrupted by any more uninvited visitors."

He almost winked as he referred to Lady Shelley and Lucia was horrified. Blushing she lowered her gaze and mumbled that she would see him later.

Lord Winterton sharply tugged on the bell before leaving the room with his hands in his pockets and whistling to himself.

Jepson came into the room and Lucia asked to be shown to her room.

"Come with me, Miss Mountford. His Lordship has arranged everything and hopes it will be to your satisfaction."

"In here, Miss Mountford," intoned Jepson, as he opened a door for her.

As Lucia walked in, a pleasant-looking girl with jet-black hair and pale skin bobbed a curtsy.

"Good afternoon, mademoiselle," she said in a pronounced French accent.

Lucia's eyes lit up.

"*Vous êtes française?*" she asked, fluently and with confidence.

"*Mais, oui, mademoiselle. Et vous parlez bien le*

français."

Jepson looked astonished and coughed nervously.

"I can see that Antoinette will look after you very well," he said. "I will leave you in her capable hands."

Lucia asked where she came from and was delighted when she told her Paris.

Very soon they were chatting away like old friends. Antoinette showed her around the room. It was large and beautifully decorated in the French style and had huge windows overlooking the garden.

Lucia ran forward and cried aloud with joy,

"A white peacock!"

"Yes, 'is Lordship is very proud of it," answered Antoinette, who had already finished unpacking Lucia's trunks. "It was shipped over from the Far East."

"I have never seen a white one before," she commented, watching it lope across the lawns. "It's so beautiful."

"I have run a bath for you, miss. In there, if you please to look."

Lucia walked over to a door that was slightly ajar. The room was full of scented steam and there were fine soaps on the basin and a pile of white towels by the bath. Everything was the height of luxury and very modern.

"I am so 'appy to be serving you," chattered Antoinette, while Lucia undressed. "I 'ave trained to be a lady's maid and I confess I was a little puzzled when 'is Lordship engaged me as he is not married. It is unusual that a secretary has a lady's maid, *non?* But Monsieur Jepson, 'e say that you are a lady yourself."

Lucia's heart sank.

'He must have asked her to look after me so that when we are married, she will continue to be my maid and be

86

familiar with my requirements,' she deduced.

"I am not strictly speaking a lady," she replied, as she eased herself into the foaming bath. "Papa was a Lord, but I am just a miss."

"Oh, I see," said Antoinette. "Boof! I shall never get used to your English Lords and Ladies. Who is Lady, who is Lord – so many!"

Lucia thought that she would very much enjoy having Antoinette to take care of her needs and she would be able to speak French more often.

The hot bath was most welcome after working so hard all day. Her shoulders and neck were stiff from pounding the typewriter keyboard and she had not realised how tense she had been.

'At least I shall have every comfort while I am here,' she thought. 'I wish though that I did not have to be away from Mama. I wonder if Lord Winterton will allow me to telephone home later this evening to see how she is?'

Later at the dressing table Antoinette brushed out her thick blonde hair and commented on how pretty it was.

"So much hair!" she said admiringly. "How shall I dress it for you?"

Lucia allowed her to style it in the French manner and found it very becoming. As she laced her into her dark-red satin dress, she thought how grown up she looked.

'Sometimes, I still feel as if I am eighteen years old,' she thought, as she admired her reflection. 'It is a pity that Papa is not here to see me.'

Just then the gong sounded for dinner.

"Come, mademoiselle. Do not keep 'is Lordship waiting."

Lucia thanked her and walked downstairs to find Jepson waiting for her.

"Good evening, Miss Mountford. His Lordship is waiting for you in the dining room," he said with a smile.

Lucia moved silently into the room and found Lord Winterton already seated. As soon as he saw her, he leapt to his feet.

"Ravishing," he said in a low voice. "I was not wrong in thinking that my first impression of you was that of an angel come down from Heaven."

Lucia felt a hot flush spread over her features that she tried hard to control. He stared at her in much the same way that he had regarded Lady Shelley earlier that afternoon and it caused her to become heated.

"It is unseasonably warm, is it not?" she said, trying to explain away her glowing features.

"I had thought it rather chill this evening," commented Lord Winterton, as he pulled out a chair for her. "I trust that the room is to your liking? It was my mother's favourite room in the house and has the best views over the gardens."

She sank down in the chair, very aware of him standing behind her. She could feel his warmth as he eased the chair in towards the table.

"Thank you, it is very nice."

"Now I have something that I wish you to have that would look perfect with that gown," he said, producing a jewellery case from his jacket.

She looked up him questioningly.

"It would please me greatly if you would wear it. It was Mama's. Consider it on permanent loan, as I hate to see beautiful jewels gathering dust. They should always be around the neck of a lovely woman."

"But I could not – "

"I want you to wear it to please me," he insisted, opening the case and taking out the necklace.

A cluster of garnets sparkled under the chandelier and Lucia could see that it was a very fine and expensive piece.

"Allow me," he volunteered in a voice that was almost a caress.

The hairs on Lucia's neck rose as his fingers brushed against her while he was doing up the catch. It sent shivers down her spine and ignited something inside her that she could not name. Whatever it was, it made her feel rather uncomfortable.

Yet, the moment he moved his fingers away, she felt strangely bereft.

He stood back and looked at her admiringly.

"Perfect!" he declared before resuming his seat, while Jepson served the soup.

The garnets glittered around her neck and she wished she could see what they looked like.

'Is it something I am doing that makes him so bold around me?' she thought, as they made polite conversation. 'Do I, in some way, encourage him?'

The soup was delicious and so was the chicken *a la crème* that followed.

"You are to be congratulated on your choice of chef," enthused Lucia as she finished. "I have not eaten such wonderful food since I was in France."

"Jepson will now serve pudding and I don't think you will be disappointed. I have heard that there are strawberries from Spain involved."

"Already?" exclaimed Lucia. "We are just into April. Surely it is too early?"

"Harrods have them shipped in from Spain. Frightfully expensive but utterly delicious. I wanted to spoil you!"

"There was really no need," replied Lucia, beginning

to feel awkward.

"Oh, you must keep your strength up for the tasks ahead," said Lord Winterton mysteriously. "Clearing my correspondence was just your first duty. Tomorrow we begin work on a project that is very dear to my heart. It will mean long hours and much hard work on your part."

"What is it?" questioned Lucia intrigued.

"I have been entrusted with a very important responsibility," he began. "It is a monument to dear friends of mine who owned an estate nearby. They went down with the *Titanic* last year – shocking business! I have managed to persuade His Majesty himself to attend the unveiling, but there is not much time. The ceremony is scheduled for the last week in June and we have much to do and little time in which to organise everything."

"*The Titanic*?" whispered Lucia.

Unable to control herself, she started shaking. Tears came unbidden and she crumpled over the dining table.

"Whatever is the matter?" he asked. "Is it something I have said?"

"Oh! You cannot know," cried Lucia. "My Papa went down in the very same ship last April. Please forgive me, but I still greatly feel the pain of our loss."

He rose and came towards her. Tenderly he put his arm round her.

"I am so sorry – I did not realise," he said gently. "Please, dry your tears."

He took his handkerchief out of his pocket and offered it to her.

"You must still be very upset. It was a terrible, terrible tragedy. The Duke and Duchess of Wantage were my friends, but I know that London lost a good many important people on that dreadful evening."

"I miss Papa a great deal," replied Lucia, feeling strangely comforted by his arm around her shoulders. "We were so close and now my Mama has remarried, I feel as if he has been forgotten."

"I am certain that your Mama has not dismissed him from her thoughts and you must not be hard on her for wishing to remarry. The world is difficult for women on their own without someone to protect them. I know Sir Arthur is different from us coming from the North, but he will always ensure that your Mama is cared for."

It was on the tip of Lucia's tongue to comment that she was not so certain that Sir Arthur would do the right thing by her mother. After all, was she not sick in bed and yet he refused her the best medical attention?

However she held her tongue and took the glass of claret he offered her.

Lord Winterton's whole manner had changed and he seemed somehow more approachable. His face was etched with concern and his eyes full of compassion.

"I have decided," he said suddenly. "We shall also dedicate the monument to your father's memory and I am certain that the new Duke will not object. He is a kind man and very compassionate as was his own father."

"You would do this for me?" she asked in wonder.

She looked into his piercing blue eyes and his warm expression touched her heart deeply. She was seeing him in a new light for the first time.

"For you and your Mama," he replied. "My dear father was fortunate enough to die in his own bed with his family all around him. The least I can do is to raise a lasting monument to honour your father's memory."

"Th-thank you," breathed Lucia. "I do not know how to thank you."

"You can work extra hard for me and that will be

enough," he said gently laying his warm hand on hers.

Lucia did not resist. It felt so comforting and protective.

She looked up him and, for one split second, she thought she saw him lean slightly towards her, as if approaching for a kiss.

In the heat of the moment she did not want to resist and she waited for his lips to alight upon hers.

But with a slight intake of breath Lord Winterton moved away and rose from the table.

Lucia felt a lurching sensation in her stomach as the disappointment stung her heart.

'I would not have resisted,' she told herself incredulously. '*I would not have resisted.*'

Her head was still reeling when she finally took her leave and returned to her room. She stared at the ceiling long into the night, trying to calm her whirling mind.

'Why does he affect me so?' she thought, desperately trying to turn her thoughts to her mother. 'I am not certain that I care to feel like this.'

*

The rest of the week soon passed for Lucia. She asked permission to use the telephone to check on her mother's progress and was told by Lord Winterton that she could use it whenever she wished.

The news from home was always very much the same – no change.

They began to work on the ceremony for the unveiling of the monument. First she had to telephone the stonemason to advise him of the changes to be made to his original design, and then, she had to draw up a list of dignitaries to attend the event.

Lord Winterton was quiet and reserved with her all

week, disappearing every so often without prior notice and reappearing just as suddenly.

"His work often takes him to London," Jepson told her, when she asked one Friday afternoon where his Lordship might be. "I never know when to expect him."

"That's a pity. I was hoping to see him before I left for the weekend. However, I shall leave him a note so that he will know what I have done so far."

"Very well, Miss Mountford. At what time shall I have the motor car brought round to the front for you?"

"Five o'clock please, Jepson, and thank you for helping me through my first week. It has been – an interesting experience."

"Oh, life is never dull when his Lordship is at home," said Jepson with a smile.

Lucia knew that he was referring to Lady Shelley. She had not made another appearance, although at every meal Lucia half expected her to sweep into the room in a cloud of heavy perfume, demanding to see Lord Winterton alone.

She was surprised how she felt to be leaving the Manor later that afternoon.

She climbed into Lord Winterton's Talbot and, even though she was looking forward to seeing her mother again, she was hit by a pang of sadness.

The journey was brief and pleasant and by the time she arrived back at Bingham Hall, it was just getting dark.

"Lucia!"

She looked up to see her stepfather coming towards her and to her surprise he had a broad smile on his face.

"Lord Winterton is delighted with you," he said, as he led her inside. "I have already had a letter from him singing your praises. At this rate, I would not be surprised if the wedding announcement is made before the six months are out. Well done, Lucia. I must admit, I was concerned that you would not be suitable, but he has allayed my fears. Champion work!"

He patted her on the shoulder and walked off with a spring in his step.

'No doubt he is also thrilled to have received a cheque for twenty-five thousand pounds,' growled Lucia as she waited for Moston to bring in her case.

As he came towards her, she idly followed him up the stairs, wondering if she should go straight to her mother's room or change first.

But before she could make that decision, Mrs. Darrowby came flying down the stairs towards her and almost knocked her down.

"Miss Lucia. I am so pleased to see you," she cried.

There was something about her expression that alarmed Lucia.

"It's your Mama," she continued. "She has taken a turn for the worse and I fear she is gravely ill. I will send for the doctor, but she cannot be left alone. Will you go to her at once?"

Lucia ran upstairs and into her mother's room and noticed the odour of Friar's Balsam hanging heavy in the air.

She could hear her mother's laboured breathing.

"Lucia, is that you?" she called feebly.

"Yes, Mama, I am here. Mrs. Darrowby has gone to fetch the doctor."

"Doctor Glossop?"

"No, Mama. Doctor Maybury will come quickly whereas Doctor Glossop may not be able to reach here until the morning."

She wheezed and coughed and how it pained Lucia to see her so ill.

As she waited for Mrs. Darrowby, Moston appeared with a letter on a tray.

"I am sorry, miss, but this came today and the messenger said it was urgent."

Lucia took the letter and immediately recognised the handwriting.

'Edward – ' she whispered to herself. 'I had quite forgotten that he asked for an answer by tomorrow. Oh, what does he want now?'

She opened it and read quickly,

"*My dearest, I hope you have not forgotten your promise to give me an answer to my proposal. With this in mind, I would ask if I might call on you tomorrow afternoon. Please telephone me at Greensides, my country home, in the morning.*

Yours, Edward."

'So he is coming up from London,' she murmured.

At that moment, her mother let out a low groan. Mrs. Darrowby came rushing back into the room with her eyes staring.

"Is she all right, miss? The doctor will be here soon. I have asked him to hurry."

As Mrs. Darrowby bustled around the room, Lucia moved closer to her mother and took her hand. She coughed again and Lucia gave her a drink.

"The doctor is on his way, Mama," she told her soothingly. "And I am here."

As her mother lay there breathing hard, Lucia prayed with all her might that the doctor would arrive before it was too late.

'Oh, Mama. Do not die,' she begged holding her hand tightly. 'Papa, if you have any influence in Heaven, don't let the Lord take her, *please*!'

CHAPTER SEVEN

Lucia sat by her mother's bedside table, waiting for Doctor Maybury to arrive. When eight o'clock arrived, Mrs. Darrowby brought her a tray of sandwiches and tea.

"Thank you so much. Is there still no sign of Doctor Maybury? Mama is getting restless as she thinks he's not coming."

"Even the Master is pacing up and down the hall, miss! I shouldn't want to be in Doctor Maybury's shoes when he does finally turn up!"

Lucia was relieved that Sir Arthur appeared at last to be showing some outward signs of concern for her mother.

Eventually, at half-past eight, they heard the front door bell ring and Moston brought Doctor Maybury upstairs.

The old man doddered through the door with his glasses perched on the end of his nose and a black bag in his hand.

Lucia thought he looked as if he was in need of medical attention himself.

"Now, now, Lady Mountford," he began, as he had obviously forgotten her remarriage. "What is the trouble?"

"Mama is finding it difficult to breathe and her cough is terrible!" intervened Lucia before her mother could speak.

Doctor Maybury examined her and dithered round her

bed.

"Hmm, her temperature appears to be somewhat higher," he muttered, as he looked at the thermometer. "And she is having more difficulty breathing."

'Heavens,' thought Lucia becoming annoyed. 'I have already told him that and I am not a doctor!'

"What can you give her to help her rest more easily?" she asked as calmly as she could.

"I have some linctus in my bag that may help. It is stronger than the last one I gave her."

He opened his bag and pulled out a brown bottle. He set it down on the bedside table and immediately Lucia picked it up and examined the label.

Satisfied that it was a fairly innocuous blend that could be bought in any village shop, she asked Mrs. Darrowby to fetch a glass of hot water.

"Doctor Glossop always used to say it does far more good if you mix cough medicine in hot water – do you remember, Mrs. Darrowby?"

She nodded with a complicit smile and Lucia knew that she shared her belief that Doctor Maybury was an old fool who should retire.

"I shall go now, Lady Mountford," bellowed Doctor Maybury, who was a little deaf as well as unsteady on his feet. "I will speak to your husband and advise him further. Good night."

He left the room and Lucia heard the sound of voices in the hall but, even though Doctor Maybury was speaking loudly, she could not quite hear what he said.

As soon as she heard the front door close, she ran downstairs.

"Stepfather," she called. "What did he say?"

He wore a grave expression and an icy shot of fear

gripped her heart.

"I am afraid we must prepare ourselves for the worst," he said solemnly. "Doctor Maybury says he does not think he can do a great deal more for her."

"No! *No!*" cried Lucia, throwing her hands up to her pale face. "It *cannot* be."

"I have thought it through and there is only one course of action," added Sir Arthur. "Although I am now in receipt of the money from Lord Winterton, nearly all of it has been swallowed up paying our creditors. I know that he is acquainted with a brilliant chest specialist from Switzerland who may be able to help."

"Then we must ask him how to contact him at once," exclaimed Lucia.

"He will not be cheap, Lucia. I'm not certain that we have the money to pay for him."

"But you must! You must! You cannot let her – *die!*"

"I shall think it through," answered Sir Arthur. "I care a great deal for your Mama and I do not intend to lose her so soon after our wedding."

"I will ask Lord Winterton if he will help us. You said that he was delighted with how I performed my duties and he has just said that I should be prepared to work long hours on a new project. Perhaps he would lend us the money to pay for the Swiss doctor if I offer to work at weekends."

"I don't think he would deny you anything. He seems very impressed with you."

Lucia bade him goodnight and returned to her mother's side and sat up all night and even found herself nodding off. She appeared to be breathing more easily and coughing less.

The clock in the hall struck half-past five and she knew that soon the servants would be up and about. She stretched out and checked her mother once again.

'Still peaceful,' she whispered and arose to ring for Mrs. Darrowby.

It had utterly escaped her mind that Edward would be visiting later that day to obtain her answer to his proposal.

*

Lucia could barely keep her eyes open by the time Mrs. Darrowby arrived.

"I'll take over now, miss. You look as if you are dead on your feet."

"Would you ask Mary-Anne to wake me up for a late luncheon?" she said, concealing a yawn with her hand.

As soon as she laid her head on the pillow, she fell into a deep sleep.

In fact when Mary-Anne came to wake her some hours later, she felt as if she had only just dropped off.

"Is it time for luncheon already?" she asked sleepily.

"Well, no, miss – " answered Mary-Anne haltingly.

"Then, why on earth have you woken me?"

"Mr. de Redcliffe is downstairs waiting to see you. I told him that you were asleep, but he was terribly insistent. He would not take no for an answer and said that you were expecting him. He became quite cross with me, he did."

It was then that Lucia remembered her promise to him.

"He is quite correct – he does have an appointment to see me. I had just forgotten. Will you go downstairs and ask him if he would not mind waiting? I shall not be long."

Mary-Anne put down the fresh pile of underclothes on the bed and left the room immediately.

'Oh, goodness! I wish I had had the presence of mind to telephone him at Greensides last night to put off his visit,' she thought, 'I am too tired to have to explain myself.'

It was only half-past eleven and Lucia wondered if she would be able to be rid of him before luncheon.

Ten minutes later, she walked into the drawing room and she thought that Edward looked rather pale too and wondered if it was the result of a sleepless night.

"Lucia!" he cried, moving quickly towards her.

She allowed him to kiss her hand and then quickly withdrew it.

"Would you care for some tea? I do apologise for keeping you waiting. Mama is still not at all well."

"Oh, I am so sorry, and I assume that now you will not wish to go for a ride this morning? In any case, it is now rather late."

"Would you mind terribly, Edward?" she said, turning her sad, grey eyes on him. "I do not feel strong enough to go haring over fields today as I had to sit up with Mama all last night."

"Do you not have servants to do that kind of thing?" asked Edward with a genuinely shocked look on his face.

"I wished to do it myself," replied Lucia quietly. "Besides, I have not seen her all week having been at Longfield Manor."

Edward took a deep breath and Lucia winced. She knew what he was about to say before the words had spilled from his mouth.

"Lucia, I hope you have had time to consider my proposal?" he asked quite brusquely.

She cast her eyes down and wrung her hands.

"Edward, I am afraid I cannot think of marriage while Mama is so ill. It would not be right. Doctor Maybury thought – "

She swallowed hard afraid that she was about to cry.

"He thought that she might not recover."

Edward nodded his head soberly. His mouth pursed in barely concealed disappointment.

"Naturally," he said at last. "You must not give it further thought. We shall talk again on a more suitable occasion. But I must warn you – I am not a man to give up easily."

He went to get up and Lucia felt alarmed that she had offended him.

"Edward, Moston has not brought our tea yet."

"There is no need for tea," answered Edward. "I can see you are very preoccupied at the moment."

Finally he rose and strode into the hall, asking a surprised Moston for his hat.

He turned briefly to bid goodbye to Lucia and left.

After he had gone, Lucia asked Moston to bring the tea tray into the drawing room.

As she sat and sipped her tea, she thought long and hard. In her heart, she knew that the next time that Edward proposed to her, she would have to search for another excuse to refuse him.

She did not care to admit that since spending so much time with Lord Winterton, she had begun to question more closely the nature of her attachment to Edward.

*

Lucia took a walk around the garden that afternoon and, as she did so, she rehearsed what she would say to Lord Winterton on Monday morning.

She did not care if they ended up owing him more money or if she had to answer a thousand letters from love-struck women, she would ask about the Swiss doctor her stepfather had mentioned.

'Surely, if we already owe him a great deal of money, then another hundred pounds or so will not make the slightest bit of difference?' she told herself, as she examined the wisteria for signs of budding flowers.

She had a whole speech formulated by dinner that evening, and announced to her stepfather that she would broach the subject with Lord Winterton as soon as she arrived at Longfield Manor on Monday.

"Oh, I'm not certain it is such a good idea," Sir Arthur told her, shaking his head. "I'm in the man's debt enough as it is and it pains me to be so."

"But Stepfather, you yourself said that Doctor Maybury has told us to prepare for the worst! You cannot let her – "

Sir Arthur sighed and picked up his soup spoon.

"Lucia. I do not want you to think that I am a heartless man. I know I am bluff at times, but I care a great deal for your Mama. Perhaps this doctor will visit us and allow us to delay payment. There is word in the City that the fortunes of my mines in South Africa may be about to improve. We must not set our hopes too high, but if they discover diamonds, we shall not want for a very long time."

"Oh, then I pray it happens!" cried Lucia passionately. "Is it likely?"

"I could not say, but we should not dwell on it in case the mines yield nothing but dirt and rock. Don't count your chickens as my mother would say."

Lucia agreed and set about her soup.

"By the way, I saw Edward de Redcliffe leaving the house again this morning. I hope you're not encouraging him? You must not forget that you are promised to Lord Winterton – he will not be pleased if he thinks that someone else is paying you attention."

"He is just a friend," sighed Lucia.

It was not an outright lie after all.

'Oh, what shall I do about Edward?' she pondered, as they ate in silence. 'I do like him, but – *marriage*?'

As the meal progressed, she told herself that she should concentrate on her mother rather than him.

'She needs me more than he does. I must find a way to persuade Lord Winterton to engage this doctor as soon as possible.'

*

Her mother appeared to neither worsen nor improve over the course of the weekend. Lucia could not wait for Monday morning and was ready waiting for Briggs to take her in the motor car at the crack of dawn.

"I want to be there early so that I can begin work on a very important project for Lord Winterton," she told him, as they sped towards Longfield Manor.

Lord Winterton was eating breakfast when she arrived and he emerged from the dining room with a puzzled expression on his face.

"So keen?" he said, an amused smile playing about his lips.

"Well, you did say that we would have to work long and hard on the unveiling ceremony, so here I am!"

"Would you care to have some breakfast first?" he asked, pushing back a lock of thick dark hair.

It was a gesture that he performed in such a languorous manner, it was as if he was attempting a seduction.

He stood awaiting her reply whilst Lucia simply blushed and handed her hat to Jepson.

"I would probably like something to eat later, but for now, I wish to make an early start."

Lord Winterton laughed in his easy manner and followed her with his eyes as she walked along the corridor.

'Damn fine girl,' he muttered appreciatively.

Lucia settled herself down at the desk and began to look through the morning's correspondence.

After a while, Lord Winterton came sauntering into the study.

"How is your mother?" he asked, as he leaned against a bookcase.

"She is not at all well, I'm afraid," replied Lucia, with emotions welling up inside her. "We had to call the doctor out again, but he was not much use. However, my stepfather mentioned that you knew of a Swiss chest specialist."

"Doctor Heidweg? Splendid fellow! Shall I telephone him and ask him to call on her?"

Lucia hung her head.

"There is just one problem. We cannot afford to pay for him. I wonder if there might be any way you could perhaps ask him to defer payment of his account until we find ourselves in better circumstances."

Lord Winterton strode across to the telephone, picked it up and waited for the exchange to answer.

"You must let me settle the account," he said, as he was put through.

"I could not hear of such a thing and nor will my stepfather."

Secretly, she was hoping that he would argue with her.

"Nonsense! Ah, Doctor Heidweg, please. Lord Winterton calling."

Lucia felt a glow of happiness as Lord Winterton quickly made arrangements for the doctor to attend her mother. After he had finished the call, he turned and came to kneel beside her.

"There, it is done," he told her in a low voice. "He will call on her this evening once his clinic in London has finished for the day. I am certain that he will be able to help her. He is a very gifted man."

"Thank you so very much," whispered Lucia, unable to meet his brilliant blue gaze. "You do not know what this means to me. How can I ever thank you?"

His voice became even lower and huskier as he replied,

"What is maybe another hundred pounds on top of the money I have already loaned Sir Arthur? In any case, I already have a down payment from him in the form of a very beautiful secretary! I will just have to make you work overtime for me!"

Lucia met his eyes and for a moment she felt that familiar tremor inside her. He did not drop his gaze and his hand crept towards hers across the desk.

In a split second, she pulled herself together and began to type.

Lord Winterton rose with an almost disappointed look on his face and for the rest of the morning, Lucia sensed a distinct tension between them.

Lord Winterton seemed to load each word with a sigh and took every opportunity to brush against her.

'Is he attempting to seduce me?' she wondered, as they left the dining room after luncheon.

He had been incredibly attentive and had flirted with her in front of Jepson.

'Does he now believe that because he has granted my family another favour, that he can expect some repayment in kind from me?'

He kept up his subtle assault all week.

By the time that Friday afternoon came, Lucia's mind was spinning with his advances. She was terrified that she might succumb to his charms.

'If only he was a good deal older and less attractive,'

she told herself, as he passed close behind her chair in the study. 'It would be easy for me to dismiss him or ignore him.'

But his overpowering masculinity was working its magic upon her.

She found herself gazing at his fine form and admiring his broad shoulders or thinking that his eyes were almost hypnotic in the way they engaged her.

And there was so much to do for the unveiling ceremony. She had to write to a huge list of dignitaries, as well as deal with the King's private secretary.

As the week drew to a close, Lucia was quite pleased with herself at how much she had achieved.

It was now late on Friday afternoon and she had almost finished her work.

Lord Winterton had just rung for some tea when none other than Lady Shelley swept into the study unannounced.

"Really, Richard," she scolded. "The front door was open – you should order your servants to be more careful."

Lucia sighed inwardly as Lady Shelley cocked her head on one side flirtatiously, whilst fluttering her eyelashes at Lord Winterton.

"Camilla, I'm busy."

Lady Shelley completely ignored him and instead made a beeline for Lucia.

"My dear, I hear that congratulations are in order."

Lucia's mouth fell open. Surely she could not know of the deal with Lord Winterton? She decided that she must bluff.

"I am sorry, Lady Shelley, but you are mistaken. I am not engaged."

Lady Shelley raised one elegant eyebrow.

"Really? That is not what I heard and that is not what

a certain Mr. de Redcliffe is telling his friends either. My brother is a close intimate of his and apparently they were discussing you at length over dinner last night."

Lucia was horrified.

'How could he?' she thought. 'How dare he tell people we are engaged when I have yet to give him an answer! I am seeing him in another light if this is true.'

Tears filling her eyes, she excused herself and ran out of the room into the corridor. She did not stop until she reached the back door that led into the garden.

"Oh dear, I seem to have upset your little secretary," commented Lady Shelley without a hint of remorse, as Lucia pushed past her.

Outside in the garden, Lucia cried hot tears of anger that not even the sight of an albino peacock could stem.

'Be sensible now, Lucia,' she told herself, as she pulled herself together. "Is it likely that Edward would discuss such personal matters with others? But how did she even know his name, let alone that he has been courting me, if she had not been told? No one except for Emmeline, Cecily and Tristram know that we have been seeing each other.'

But she doubted that any of her friends would even know about Edward's proposal.

'I will write to him this evening and ask him outright,' she decided. 'He is far too upright to fib, but I hope Lady Shelley is now satisfied with the mischief she has made and what will Lord Winterton think of me now? That the woman who he has struck a marriage deal with is a trollop who gets herself engaged to other men?'

Lucia suddenly realised how very much she did care about what Lord Winterton thought of her and that she felt more for him than just admiration.

'For the time being, I must seek to limit the amount of damage that stupid woman has done,' she said to herself, returning to the house.

However, when she returned to the study, it was empty. Although the scent of Lady Shelley's heavy perfume still lingered, there was no sign of anyone. She listened to see if she could hear sounds from the library next door, but all was silent.

'It's just as if they had vanished into thin air.'

She had not been back in the study for long when Jepson came in to announce that the motor car was being brought round for her.

"Is it time already?" she said, looking at the clock on the mantelpiece.

"Yes, Miss Mountford. Shall I ask the driver to wait for you?"

"Please," she answered, feeling a little flustered. She was looking forward to seeing her mother again, as the reports back from the Hall had so far been highly encouraging.

When she had telephoned the day before, Mrs. Darrowby had said that her mother had made a marked improvement. Not only that, but Doctor Heidweg was calling on her every other day.

She willed the motor car along the roads to Bingham Hall and soon, they were travelling up the drive to the house.

As soon as they arrived, she jumped out and ran straight upstairs.

To her delight her Mama was indeed looking much better.

"How is she?" she asked Mrs. Darrowby.

"A great deal better than she was. Doctor Heidweg has prescribed some strange cures. We have to give her all manner of baths and inhalants, but they appear to be working."

"Yet, she still sleeps?"

"He says she must rest to recover her strength. I just wish she would eat a little more and then I would be happy."

Lucia kissed her sleeping mother and went to change.

As soon as Mary-Anne had helped her dress for dinner, she sat down and wrote to Edward. In her letter she described her displeasure at Lady Shelley's disclosure and asked him for an explanation.

"If it is true, what she says she found out from your brother, then you must know there is no chance that I would accept your proposal and will not wish to see you again," she wrote fiercely.

The gong sounded before she had the opportunity to finish, so she put down her pen and sighed.

'I shall continue with this later. In any case it cannot be posted until tomorrow.'

But later that evening, after she had put the finishing touches to her letter to him, she lay in bed and tried to imagine what it would be like to be married to Edward.

To her shock each time she attempted to picture them together, it was not Edward who manifested himself in her fantasy, but Lord Winterton!

'I must stop this nonsense,' she told herself crossly, thumping her fists into the soft feather mattress.

Even more worrying, she could not help but fantasise about how her wedding night might unfold, if it was Lord Winterton she had ended up marrying, rather than Edward de Redcliffe!

'It's all his fault. His bad influence is causing me to have such unnatural thoughts,' she sighed, pushing her face into the pillow.

She awoke the next morning feeling quite exhausted, but she tried not show her tiredness as she walked in to see her mother.

"Lucia," she called. "I must have been asleep when you returned home yesterday. I must say, this new doctor is wonderful. I am feeling a great deal better."

"You must continue to rest," counselled Lucia, smoothing down her hair. "Mrs. Darrowby tells me that he has said you must not exert yourself."

"I like him much more than that old fool from the village, although I must say that some of his methods seem a little eccentric."

"I'm certain he knows what he's doing," replied Lucia. "Now, you must try and eat some breakfast for me. Maybe a little toast. Nice and soft with butter."

She kissed her mother on the forehead and then went downstairs. In her pocket was the letter for Edward.

At the foot of the stairs, she gave it to Moston asking for it to be sent at once.

'There, it is done,' she said to herself. 'I think I will go for a drive after breakfast. I need to think and to clear my head.'

An hour later, she was striding towards the stables wearing her new hat and her soft, leather driving gloves.

"Briggs. Can you bring the Rolls Royce out for me, please?" she asked confidently.

"You going for a drive, miss?" he asked with a grin. "Do you want me to come with you?"

"No, thank you. I want to drive myself. I have been cooped up all week at Longridge Manor and wish to get some air in my lungs."

She jumped into the driving seat while Briggs held the door open for her.

As he helped her start the engine, she thrilled as she put her foot on the accelerator and it purred into life.

Slowly releasing the handbrake and next the clutch, the car moved forwards.

It was always at this point that Lucia felt a shiver of excitement. Concentrating on her driving, she took the car along the drive and turned left at the gates.

Soon she was speeding along the country lanes with her cares blowing behind her.

'What a beautiful day,' she thought, as the sun came out from behind a cloud and the banks shimmered with daffodils.

Turning right at the junction, she soon became lost but continued on, thinking it all a great adventure.

After a while the road came to a dead end and she realised that she was near the river.

Stopping the car she turned off the engine and climbed out.

The sun was warm and she felt quite carefree. She walked along the riverbank for a while and then sat down by a tree. Taking off her hat and gloves, she soon dozed off.

"Well, what a surprise!"

She opened her eyes with a start to find Lord Winterton standing in front of her. His horse was drinking from the river and he looked very handsome in his rust-coloured riding habit.

"Wh-what are you doing here?" she asked, equally as startled as he.

"This river borders the land I am seeking to acquire. I thought I'd take a ride out to inspect it and I must say this is quite a pleasant surprise."

Lucia jumped up as if she had been stung.

'I must get away quickly,' she said to herself.

Suddenly without the comforting familiarity of the walls of Longridge Manor around her, Lucia felt incredibly vulnerable.

"Where are you going?" he asked, catching hold of her arm.

"I – I must return to the Hall. Mama – "

"How is she?"

"She has improved, thank you."

Lord Winterton stood there, still holding on to her arm. His blue eyes burned into her face and she noticed him lick his lips beneath his clipped moustache.

They remained staring into each other's eyes for a few seconds and then Lord Winterton suddenly pulled her towards him and his urgent mouth was on hers, kissing her in a manner she had never experienced.

She felt something inside of her soar before realising what she was doing.

"*No!*" she cried, pulling away – her face red and her head reeling from the kiss. "Let me go!"

"I am so sorry, I don't know what came over me," said Lord Winterton. "Forgive me, Lucia, I was lost in the moment."

Without waiting to reply, Lucia ran towards the car, jumped in and started the engine. With a swift turn of the wheel, she manoeuvred the car back along the bank and onto the road again.

'If I needed further proof of how his loose morals have infected me, then I have just had it,' she scolded herself, as she drove like the wind back to Bingham Hall. 'I will speak to my stepfather the moment I return and see if this terrible arrangement cannot be cancelled at once. I don't care, I cannot marry the man. He is no good – *no good at all*.'

CHAPTER EIGHT

Lucia was still really upset by the time she turned the Rolls Royce into the drive of Bingham Hall.

Briggs could not contain his astonishment as she leapt out of the motor car, leaving the engine still running.

Hot tears of anger ran down Lucia's face as she swept inside.

'Now my day has been ruined,' she fumed, running up the stairs to her bedroom.

She washed her face and then went in search of Sir Arthur. Unfortunately, he was out and Moston seemed to think that he would not be returning until dinner.

Lucia was left to her own devices.

Although she should have been happy to be home, she now felt so restless and ill at ease that she did not know what to do with herself.

'It is true, I enjoyed his kiss,' she admitted to herself, as she paced the gardens. 'But it is wrong. I know that I am promised to him, but I wish I could persuade my stepfather that it would not be right for me to marry a man with such loose morals. I do not care for the effect that he has on me and I do not believe he would make a good husband.'

There was also the problem of Edward.

Lucia wondered how quickly he would receive her

letter. She knew that he had told her he would be at Greensides, but what if he had changed his mind and had returned to London?

'Oh, I wish I could just run away,' she thought, as she sat down on a stone bench overlooking the fountains. 'But with Mama so unwell, I would not dare.'

She ruminated and not for the first time, that if her father had never met Sir Arthur McAllister, not only would he still be alive, but she would not now be facing her current predicament.

'Then, it would simply be a matter of whether I cared enough to accept Edward's proposal and nothing more,' she mused. 'Papa would have known what I should do.'

To keep herself occupied, she sat with her mother until dinner. She was looking brighter and feeling well enough to listen to Lucia reading aloud to her.

"Mama, I have some news you may care to hear. Lord Winterton has been charged with the responsibility of raising a monument to an important local couple who went down with the *Titanic* and he has now said that he will include Papa's likeness and name on the monument. The King is to unveil it."

"That is indeed wonderful news. It does not seem possible that a year has passed and to think, I will be too ill lying in my bed to visit the cemetery."

Her mother sighed again.

"Will you have Moston put some flowers around your father's picture on the landing on the anniversary? And ask that the candles should remain alight all that day and the next."

"Of course, Mama," replied Lucia. "Perhaps I should ask Lord Winterton for time off to visit the cemetery."

"I'm still not happy about your working for him. Why do you have to?"

"Because Stepfather has borrowed a great deal of money from him and I am providing him a service until such time as the debt is repaid. Besides, I don't mind working."

"But we are gentlewomen – we do not work!" her mother answered horrified. "To think a daughter of mine lives in such reduced circumstances."

"It is the modern way, Mama. Lots of women now find gainful employment to occupy themselves. It is no longer the fashion to be idle, even if one has the means."

"I don't understand, you speak as if you were one of those hideous Suffragettes!"

Lucia laughed.

"I don't think that because I work, it makes me a Suffragette, Mama."

"I am glad to hear it. Your stepfather would be very angry if he thought he was harbouring one under his roof. Lucia looked at the clock and thought that it was time that she dressed, so she rang for Mrs. Darrowby and left her mother in her capable hands.

She was not looking forward to the conversation ahead.

She felt she had to inform her stepfather of Lord Winterton's advances and of the fact that he persisted in entertaining a married woman.

At the sound of the gong, she walked downstairs, trying hard to calm herself as she took each step.

Sir Arthur was already seated when she entered the room. He was always very punctual for meals and became angry if others were late.

"Good evening, Lucia. How are you?"

She took a deep breath.

"I am a little out of sorts, Stepfather. There is something I would wish to speak to you about."

"Oh?" he replied, not appearing very interested.

"It is Lord Winterton. I believe his character is questionable."

"Nonsense, he is a fine man."

"Stepfather, he entertains a married woman in private. And I have reason to believe that their liaison is not – proper."

"Lucia, I grow weary of your attempts to extricate yourself from the bargain I have struck. I had thought, because of the favourable reports I have had from Lord Winterton, that you had become accustomed to your fate. Attempting to blacken his character will not make me change my mind. I am indebted to him enormously and you know the terms of our arrangement."

"But Stepfather – "

Lucia looked at him pleadingly, but Sir Arthur's face turned puce and he slammed down his fork.

"Lucia, I warn you. Do not arouse my ire!"

"But today he tried to kiss me and I don't care for how he conducts himself!"

"Dammit, girl! You are almost betrothed to him!" he shouted, so loudly that Moston jumped. His eyes bulged and spittle hung from his lips.

Lucia had never seen him so angry.

"He is entitled to kiss you if he so wishes!" he fumed, barely pausing for breath. "What did you expect? He is not a lily-livered boy – he is accustomed to taking what he wants. No, you will go to the Manor on Monday as arranged. Do you want your mother to die? If you anger Lord Winterton and he refuses to pay for your mother's doctor's account, then that is just what will happen."

Subdued, Lucia sat in silence while Moston served dinner, her appetite all but vanished.

Dinner was an interminable affair that evening and all Lucia wished to do was return to her room. Eventually when the meal was over, she excused herself.

As she made her way into the hall, she asked Moston if there had been any messages or telephone calls for her.

"No, miss. Are you expecting something?"

"Yes. If Mr. de Redcliffe telephones or a letter arrives, I want you to come and find me at once."

"Very good, Miss Lucia."

'It is most strange that he has not replied,' she thought, as Mary-Anne helped her undress. 'Perhaps he has gone to London after all. In which case, by the time he responds, I may well be back at Longridge Manor. Oh! I am no nearer solving this mystery.'

As she tucked herself up for the night, try as she might, she could not help but relive each second of Lord Winterton's kiss.

It made her feel so strange and full of longing that she tossed and turned until the small hours of the morning.

'He is in my blood and I don't care for it. I wish I could run away from him and it would all be much better if I could!'

*

The next day Lucia occupied herself with domestic matters as her mother's illness had meant that the monthly household accounts had been left undone.

There were also the staff wages to be made up and the inventories to go through, giving Lucia barely a moment to herself.

So by the time that the evening came, she was quite tired.

"I think I shall have dinner in my room this evening, Moston," she ordered wearily. "Just something light, please, and will you inform my stepfather that I will not be joining him?"

"Of course, Miss Lucia."

Lucia sighed and was about to drag herself up the staircase when the telephone rang. Even before Moston reached it to answer it, she knew who it was.

"It's Mr. de Redcliffe, miss. Are you at home?"

Lucia walked towards him and took the phone from his hand.

"Edward, how are you?"

"Lucia! If it was not so late, I would come over at once," he replied in a desperate tone. "Your letter – I do not know what to say except that I have only met this Lady Shelley once and that was at a ball I attended with Anthony, her brother."

"But she knew that you had proposed to me. Edward, be honest with me – have you been discussing this with her brother?"

"No, I swear!" cried Edward. "I have simply no idea how she knows. Anthony does know that I have been calling on you, but I promise you, I have not said a word to him about my intentions. You *must* believe me."

Lucia did not doubt the truth behind his words – after all, had she not said that he was incapable of telling a lie?

"Very well, we shall forget the matter," she replied coolly.

"Please tell me that all is well between us. I could not bear it if I thought I had created a breach between us."

"Do not concern yourself, Edward. Nothing has altered."

"Then, say you will have dinner with me next weekend."

After a long pause, Lucia confirmed that she would

and bade him goodnight.

'Well, this is a fine mystery,' she pondered, as she closed her bedroom door. 'I can only assume that Lady Shelley has simply taken a lucky stab, having heard that Edward and I have been seen out together. No doubt, she is jealous of my closeness to Lord Winterton and seeks to create a division between us. He could not have told her of his arrangement with my stepfather, otherwise, she would have created even more trouble!'

Sitting down in her chair, she looked out of the window at the disappearing sun and wondered what lay in wait for her that week at Longridge Manor.

*

The Rolls Royce was ready and waiting for her early on Monday morning. Lucia climbed in feeling exhausted. She had spent another restless night, trying to expunge visions of Lord Winterton from her mind. Even in her dreams, he pursued her, his hot red mouth seeking hers and his hands caressing her face and sliding down to her waist –

'I don't think I can face him," she thought, as they arrived at Longridge Manor. Her heart was beating inordinately fast as she stepped out of the motor car.

But to her surprise, when she met him in the study, he was quiet and respectful. He did not try and stand too close to her, or make love with his words. Instead, he was friendly, but businesslike.

Half of her was relieved whilst the other half wondered what on earth he might be thinking. Their schedule of work was rather heavy and there was so much to do and so little time in which to achieve it.

"Today, Mr. Hopkirk, the stonemason, is arriving at half-past eleven to show us a model of the monument," Lord Winterton told her, striding around the study.

Lucia thought he looked very handsome in his dark

suit and in spite of herself, her heart quickened as she listened to his rich low voice.

"This is a most important event for me, Lucia," he said intensely. "I want us both to work exceedingly hard together so that everything is perfect. We cannot let His Majesty down – he is expecting a great deal from us."

Later that week, King George's private secretary visited the Manor.

"His Majesty has asked me to convey to you how very much he is looking forward to this event," he said. "I trust you will not disappoint us."

Lord Winterton shook his hand earnestly and rang for Jepson. After the man had left, he threw himself on the sofa in the study and splayed out his fine strong legs.

Lucia had to turn her eyes away otherwise she would have continued to stare at him.

All week she found it very difficult not to allow her gaze to linger too long on his face and form. The weather had turned warm and he had shed his jacket. His waistcoat fitted him so tightly that she could not help but admire his shape.

All too soon, Friday came and Lucia found herself quite sad to be leaving. She was also thoroughly perplexed at the change in his attitude towards her.

There had been no careless words, no long gazes and he had kept a respectful distance.

As the footman loaded his motor car with her bags, Lord Winterton took her to one side.

"There is one matter I wish to discuss with you. I think I owe you an apology for my conduct of last weekend. It was wrong of me to act so offensively and I ask your forgiveness."

"It is all forgotten," answered Lucia, feeling awkward.

"Now, I must make haste back to the Hall. I am anxious to see Mama. Mrs. Darrowby said that Doctor Heidweg is still very pleased with her progress."

As she turned to move away, Lord Winterton caught hold of her hand. For one moment, she thought he would squeeze it, but instead, it brought it to his lips and kissed it.

"Please convey my regards to your mother," he requested in a husky voice.

Lucia could not look him in the eye as she climbed into the motor car.

Her flesh felt as if it had been singed by his kiss. The imprint of it burned as the car took off down the drive. She did not dare look back, so she simply stared at her white hand, half expecting to find a mark on it.

'I wish I did not feel like this,' she thought, biting her lip.

Indeed her heart lurched as the Talbot turned out of the driveway and headed back towards Bingham Hall.

*

It did not surprise her, on returning home, to find a letter from Edward, asking if she would still care to dine at Greensides that Saturday evening.

She ran upstairs and hastily composed a note of acceptance and asked Mary-Anne to have it delivered by hand first thing the next morning.

She was delighted to find her mother sitting up in bed with a good deal more colour in her cheeks.

"Lucia, I am so glad you are home again."

"You are feeling better, Mama?"

"Yes, a little. I am still very weak, but Doctor Heidweg says that is to be expected. He is a marvellous man and has worked wonders on me."

"Mama, would you mind if I dined with Emmeline

tomorrow evening?"

Lucia hated lying to her, but she did not want her to know that she was seeing Edward again. She might innocently let it slip in conversation with her stepfather and then all hell would break loose.

"Not at all, but you must ask your stepfather's permission. You know what his feelings about how he perceives the way you should behave."

"Of course, Mama," she said, casting her eyes downwards. She hated asking Sir Arthur for anything – it did not feel right.

Kissing her mother on the cheek, she went in search of him.

'I should get this over with before we sit down to dinner,' she decided.

To her surprise, he was in a good humour when she found him in the study.

He smiled in an avuncular fashion and told her to go and enjoy herself. It would do her good to see her friends.

So when she set off the following evening for Greensides, she felt a little guilty that she had told a lie.

Edward was waiting for her in his comfortable drawing room.

"You look very beautiful," he sighed, as his butler took her coat.

The conversation was rather stilted and Lucia found herself yearning for the easy discourse she usually enjoyed with Lord Winterton.

For all his other faults and questionable character traits, he was a witty and amusing gentleman with a fondness for culture.

Edward, on the other hand, talked of race meetings and the forthcoming opening of the polo season. Although she loved to ride, Lucia found horseracing interminably dull and polo even more so.

Soon she found herself stifling a yawn as the butler served the pudding.

"Shall we listen to some music after dinner?" suggested Edward.

Lucia thought that anything that did not encourage conversation, especially on certain dangerous topics, would be most welcome and so she enthusiastically said she would love to.

"I hope you like Strauss," said Edward, winding up the gramophone.

"Yes, indeed I do," she replied, closing her eyes as the music began.

Immediately, the swelling orchestra transported her and, in her mind's eye, she was dancing with Lord Winterton across a deserted ballroom and he only had eyes for her. He whirled her around in his strong capable arms and she felt as if she was dancing on air, so light were his steps.

As the music finished, she opened her eyes and came back down to earth with a bump. Edward was standing by the gramophone, fussing with a box of needles.

"I am certain that I had some loud ones in here," he muttered to himself, poking around the small oblong tin. "I shall have to ask Simpson where they are."

'Oh, he is such a fusspot!' thought Lucia, as she watched him ring for his butler and then stand over the gramophone until he entered the room.

"There is a rather special piece of music I would like to play for you this evening," he said, as Simpson flipped up the arm and replaced the needle.

"Thank you, Simpson, that will be all."

Lucia knew what Edward would do next, even before

he had placed the record on the turntable.

It was, as she suspected, a romantic piece. She was fond of Debussy, but tonight it was making her feel uncomfortable.

She was very grateful to be sitting in an armchair and not on the sofa where Edward could have installed himself next to her.

Halfway through the record, Edward advanced towards her, dropped to one knee and took her hand.

"Oh, Lucia. I do love you so," he declared, as she turned her face away. "Say you will be mine!"

The music ended and he still held her hand fast in his. The needle scraped against the grooves of the record and made a dreadful noise.

Lucia wrinkled her brow and withdrew her hand.

"For Heaven's sake, Edward – take that record off! That sound is grating on my nerves."

The irritability of her tone surprised her and his face fell.

"Of course," he agreed quietly and stood up to attend to the gramophone.

"Edward, I cannot marry you at present," she said suddenly. "Mama is not yet well enough and I am so busy with my work. Now, I am very tired, can you ask Simpson to have Briggs bring the car to the front of the house?"

He turned towards her with a disappointed expression.

Ten minutes later, he was walking her to the waiting Rolls Royce.

"Do I entertain any hope at all that you will ever accept me?" he pleaded as she climbed into the car.

Lucia did not reply. She smiled wanly at him and wished him good night.

He stood at the doorway waving to her until the car

was out of sight.

*

When Lucia arrived at Longridge Manor on Monday morning, she was surprised when Jepson informed her that his Lordship had been called away and would not be in residence for most of the week.

"He has left instructions in the study as to what needs doing," Jepson told her.

'Oh, what a nuisance!' thought Lucia, as she sat down to read his letters.

It felt strangely lonely to be at Longridge Manor without Lord Winterton and she found she missed him dreadfully.

The hours crawled by and it was not helped by a bout of rainy weather that persisted all week, preventing her from riding or walking.

Lord Winterton did not return all week and, when Lucia arrived on the following Monday, full of hope that she would see him again, he still did not appear.

It was all very mysterious.

Jepson obviously had some inkling of where he was, yet in spite of pressing him, all he would say was that his Lordship had been called away suddenly.

This state of affairs continued long into May and soon Lucia found herself with barely seven weeks left in which to complete all the arrangements.

Each day at the Manor, she arose hoping that he would return home, but by the end of the evening she was forced to give up hope of seeing him and retired.

Far from putting a distance between them, his absence was only fanning the flames of her affection.

'Oh, how I long to see him,' she mused wistfully, as she stared out of the study window one afternoon.

She had just seen the stonemason's photographs of the finished monument and she had been overwhelmed at how accurate the likeness was of her father.

'It's unfair that Lord Winterton is not here to share these small triumphs with me. I do hope he will return in time for the big day.'

She often stood in front of the painting of him in the hall and stared long and hard at the heroic portrayal of him.

'Perhaps he is not coming back,' she thought miserably, gazing up at his likeness.

She longed to stroke those familiar features and quite shocked herself by thinking how she would like to cover them with kisses on his return.

Lucia went through the motions of work each day, but increasingly found she had not the same heart for it as when Lord Winterton had been present.

Then, one Friday evening, she returned home to Bingham Hall to find everyone in a high state of excitement.

Moston was smiling for the first time in months and she noticed that there were new items in the hall and drawing room.

'How very strange!' she thought, picking up a new and expensive-looking porcelain vase that now replaced the chipped one that used to stand in the hall.

She was just examining a new oil painting of a steam engine, when Sir Arthur emerged from the library.

"Lucia, you are back early today. Do you like that painting? I bought it in London earlier in the week."

Lucia thought he had taken leave of his senses.

'Where is the money coming from for such luxuries?' she thought.

"I'm glad I have caught you before dinner," he continued. "Would you mind coming to the library for a moment? There is something I need to discuss with you."

"Mama – she has not taken a turn for the worst?" she answered anxiously, thinking it strange that he sought to speak to her in private.

"No, to the contrary. She is so much better and Mrs. Darrowby has even taken to wheeling her around the garden in her bath chair."

'Then, I wonder what on earth he wants?' she said to herself, as she followed him into the library.

"Lucia," he began, "Mr. de Redcliffe came to see me in the week to ask for your hand."

"No!" she cried, wondering why on earth he would do so when she had expressly and repeatedly asked him not to.

She braced herself for the inevitable storm of abuse, but to her surprise her stepfather appeared calm and far from angry. He took a deep breath and, when he looked at her, it was almost with pity rather than annoyance.

Lucia was utterly puzzled.

He raised his hand as if to silence her protests.

"Up until this moment, I would have sent the man packing, having promised you to Lord Winterton. But then I read something in the *Westminster Gazette* earlier in the week and I realised that Lord Winterton has no intention of carrying our bargain through to its intended conclusion.

"Furthermore this week I heard news that my gold mines in South Africa have struck the mother lode. My stake is now worth millions and to pay him back will no longer be a hardship. Lucia, I feel I should show it to you, as I now consider you released from the bargain we struck.

"You are twenty-two next month and it is high time you were married. When you have read it, I feel certain that you will be inclined to accept Mr. de Redcliffe's proposal. You will find that I will not stand in your way – in fact, you have my whole-hearted approval."

He moved away from his desk and dropped a copy of the *Westminster Gazette* onto the table.

Lucia noticed that it was open at the Society Circular page.

Not saying another word, he left the room, leaving her alone.

At first she scanned the page quickly, skipping past the announcements of births, marriages and engagements and she suddenly stopped short as she came across the News from Abroad section.

"The word that Lady Shelley, widow of the late Lord Shelley, has become engaged to Lord Winterton of Longridge Manor was the talk of Vienna this weekend. The happy couple are said to be planning a September wedding in London."

"No! *No!*" cried Lucia, tears filling her eyes and her heart breaking into pieces. "How could he? *How could he?*"

She remained in the library for some time, re-reading the newspaper, attempting to find some sense in those few words.

'No wonder he has not been home,' she thought. 'And I had thought it odd that Lady Shelley had not visited the Manor. She was with him all the time.'

Lucia felt overwhelmed and utterly foolish.

'To think I had believed myself to be in love with him!' she howled, castigating herself for such idiocy. 'Perhaps that is his art – he makes people fall in love with him in order to get what he wants. Well, I shall not sit around waiting for them to come home and laugh at us all for having pulled the wool over our eyes!'

Still holding the newspaper in her hand, she rose and strode out of the room to the telephone in the hall. Picking it up, she waited for the exchange to answer.

'Yes,' she murmured to herself, 'I know what I must do now.'

"Good afternoon, Miss Mountford, which number do you require?"

Lucia took a deep breath before replying. She had made her mind up and nothing was going to stop her.

"Mayfair 212, please."

She waited on the line while she was connected. At last, the phone began to ring at the other end and Lucia heard Edward de Redcliffe's voice answer.

"Edward? This is Lucia."

"Lucia, how wonderful to hear from you."

"There is something I wish to say to you."

"Lucia, do not be cross with me. I thought that if I did not ask your stepfather for your hand, you might never accept. At least, I thought if the old man doesn't approve, then I shall just jolly well forget the whole thing."

"Edward, I am not cross with you," she answered, in a voice that was ice-like in its composure. "I have rung to tell you that I have finally made my decision."

"Oh?"

"Edward, I accept your proposal. I would be glad to become your wife!"

She barely heard Edward's whoops of joy and protestations of love on the other end of the line.

Standing motionless in the hall, listening to Edward's delight, she slowly and deliberately screwed up the newspaper in her hand and dropped it on the floor.

'*There*!' she fumed, grinding it under her heel as tears streamed down her face.

CHAPTER NINE

Before Lucia knew it, champagne corks were popping for the first time in ages at Bingham Hall.

Her stepfather laid on a lavish luncheon for their friends and some close relatives. Even Sir Arthur's brother came down from Manchester for the occasion.

Lucia tried to smile at the luncheon party.

Everyone admired her engagement ring – an enormous square-cut emerald surrounded by diamonds that had been in Edward's family for generations – and said how fortunate she was to make such a good match.

The date was set for July 14th on what would have been her father's birthday.

"Sir Arthur seems very happy," Moston said to Lucia, "and I am so pleased that your mother appears to be making a full recovery."

Indeed her mother was up and dressed in one of her best gowns for the occasion. From the moment that the engagement was announced, she had declared that she would make certain that she would be able to attend the luncheon.

"Yes," replied Lucia. "It's a big day for us all. Stepfather is, once again, exceedingly rich, thanks to his diamond mines in South Africa."

She could not tell him how much she missed Lord Winterton or that her heart hurt deeply whenever she thought about him.

'Edward is a good man,' Lucia had told herself. 'He will make a far better husband than Lord Winterton ever could and he will not humiliate me by maintaining a string of mistresses!'

Lord Winterton's name had not been mentioned in Bingham Hall since the day Sir Arthur had told Lucia about the article in the *Westminster Gazette*. In fact no one had heard from Lord Winterton at all.

Lucia now only went to Longridge Manor a few days each week, as word soon spread around that he was abroad and unlikely to accept any invitations.

A slight hiccup had occurred with the unveiling ceremony. The King's private secretary had contacted Lucia to ask if the whole event could be postponed until the third week of July.

In some ways, Lucia was grateful. She quickly arranged for her mother to attend in her place, thus sparing her the humiliation of having to see Lord Winterton and she pressed Edward to book their honeymoon for the same time.

"But Venice in July is hellish!" complained Edward.

"Then we shall go somewhere else. Anywhere, as long as I am not in England, I don't care."

"I would hope that as long as we were together you would not care where we went," commented Edward sadly.

Immediately Lucia had felt shamed.

"Of course," she had answered. "That goes without saying."

And now she was finding it very hard to maintain a façade of being the happy bride-to-be. Her friends were all delighted at the prospect of a July wedding and thought it all so romantic.

"I just wanted to say how thrilled I am, Lucia," her

mother told her. "To see you so well-matched is all I have ever desired and Edward is a fine young man."

Lucia squeezed her hand. How could she tell her the real reason for the wedding proceeding with such haste?

"And it is such a nice gesture that you are being married on your dear Papa's birthday. I am certain that he is up in Heaven smiling down on you. Now, one other matter, dearest. Have you handed in your notice at Longridge Manor? Arthur tells me that since he has touched gold, he has paid off his debt and we are no longer under any obligation to *that man*."

Lucia felt tears pricking her eyes.

The fact that her mother refused to even name Lord Winterton hurt her.

'They still see him as the villain of the piece,' she thought, as she moved away to mingle with her guests. 'And how can I possibly argue with that judgement when he has behaved in such a caddish fashion? Leading me on and then fleeing the country to carouse with Lady Shelley!'

She felt bitter as well as hurt and, even though she attempted to throw herself into the party and the preparations for her wedding, her heart was not truly in it.

*

The day after the party, Lucia arose to find that her stepfather had placed an announcement in *The Times* regarding her engagement.

"See how well your two names go together?" said her mother, as she excitedly handed her the newspaper. "*Lucia Mountford and Edward de Redcliffe*. It sounds rather grand!"

"Oh, Mama, it's not as if he was an Earl or even a Baronet."

"I see that one of those damned Suffragettes has gone

and thrown herself under the King's horse," muttered Sir Arthur. "Damn silly women!"

Lucia turned the pages quickly and found the report of a Miss Emily Wilding Dawson being trampled underfoot at Tuesday's Derby race meeting.

"Goodness," declared Lucia, her eyes wide with amazement. "To think that she felt so strongly for her cause that she would do such a thing."

"I call it ridiculous! Why on earth do women want the vote when they have perfectly sane husbands to do the thinking for them? It isn't right!" bellowed Sir Arthur, so loudly that the breakfast cups on the dining table rattled. "Don't you go getting any notions in that head of yours," he said pointedly at Lucia.

"Darling, Edward would not be marrying Lucia if he felt she was of a radical persuasion," cooed her mother.

Satisfied he returned to his breakfast and did not bring up the subject again.

Lucia turned to the announcement once more and wondered if Lord Winterton would see it. She knew he was accustomed to taking *The Times*.

'And what will he think?' she asked herself, as the black and white print danced before her eyes.

"It could have been so different – " she mumbled out loud without realising it.

"What on earth is wrong?" asked her mother.

"I mean – if Emily Wilding Davison had not been so militant," replied Lucia, thinking quickly in order to cover herself. She blushed deeply and resolved to keep her feelings in check more efficiently in future.

Lucia wondered when a similar missive would appear about Lord Winterton's mooted nuptials.

'Once I see it in print I will know that there is no hope

of anything happening between us,' she determined.

"Don't forget you have a fitting with the dressmaker this afternoon," said her mother, interrupting her thoughts, as Moston helped her from her chair.

"No, Mama. I have asked Briggs to take us to London in the Rolls Royce immediately after luncheon.

"You don't know how happy I am," she whispered in Lucia's ear, as she hobbled past.

Lucia smiled back at her, but could not prevent her heart from sinking.

*

The fitting at the dressmaker's dragged on for hours and Lucia and her mother felt exhausted. They both flopped back into the Rolls Royce.

"Goodness. I felt as if I was a very large pincushion!" cried Lucia. "That French girl would insist upon trying to fasten the material to my skin."

"It will look lovely, darling. Don't you think so?" sighed her mother. "So very French and the height of fashion. I should not be surprised if people will come from miles around just to see you walk up the Church path. There will not have been such a grand wedding in the County for years."

Lucia knew her mother was looking forward to once again showing off what an important family they were.

She thought it curious that since word had spread that their fortunes were once again looking rosy, neighbours had begun to call on them again.

The announcement of the engagement to Edward had also brought people flocking to the door of Bingham Hall, some of whom Lucia had never met before.

"When we return home, I will have a nap," announced her mother. "And then I want to show you some menus for the wedding breakfast. Edward's mother has sent them and has offered us her French chef for the day. I have accepted naturally."

"Mama, do I have to have a large wedding? I am concerned that all this will place such a strain on you that you will have a relapse."

Lucia did not explain that she would prefer a smaller wedding, as she wanted as little fuss as possible.

"Nonsense, of course you must have the best that our money can buy. It sounds to me as if you are experiencing pre-wedding nerves."

"A little."

"It's only natural," added her mother soothingly. "I was the same myself before I married your Papa."

'Edward will make a good husband,' she told herself for the umpteenth time that day. 'I will not want for anything and I shall have a very nice life.'

But how she wished she could convince herself and forget about Lord Winterton!

*

The following day, Lucia drove to Longridge Manor to finish off the arrangements for the unveiling ceremony.

During the afternoon, she visited Shilborough to inspect the monument. It was already in place in the town square covered by tarpaulin and scaffolding.

The stonemason proudly showed her the relief of her father and it brought tears to her eyes.

"Thank you so much" she whispered. "It is a perfect likeness and captures exactly his noble profile."

She felt sad that she would not be able to attend the ceremony. She would have loved to have been there when the covers came off and the band struck up.

But everything had now been set into motion.

Edward had booked a week in the Swiss Alps and a fortnight at a Black Sea resort. He had said that he had heard it was where the fashionable set was now going.

Lucia liked to travel and was looking forward to seeing new places, but in her heart she still longed to see or hear news of Lord Winterton.

Arriving back at the Manor, Lucia slipped inside to attend to a few items before leaving for the day.

As she passed the oak staircase, she looked up at the painting of Lord Winterton hanging on the landing.

His piercing blue eyes stared out from the canvas and his mouth seemed even more resolute than normal.

'I miss him so much,' she sighed and then told herself off for having indulged her feelings once more.

'Is it right that I still pine for another when I am to be married in a few weeks?' she pondered, as she tidied the study. 'Perhaps this ridiculous fancy will pass once I am a married woman with a home of my own to run.'

Lucia thought that she would not possibly have time to think about Lord Winterton with both Greensides and the house in Mayfair to occupy her.

Edward had already said that he wanted Greensides redecorated and that, with her wonderful eye for detail, he wanted her to personally oversee the renovations.

And then, there would be the inevitable parties and dinners they would be expected to give once they had returned from honeymoon.

"Good afternoon, Miss Mountford," came a voice behind her.

"Good afternoon, Jepson. Is there any word from Lord Winterton?"

"We still do not know when to expect him," he answered, lowering his eyes.

A feeling in her stomach told her that he was withholding information. Did it not stand to reason that Lord Winterton's most faithful servant would be informed of his Master's comings and goings?

'He knows something,' concluded Lucia.

"I am surprised that Lady Shelley has not been to the Manor," she probed, hoping to trick him into telling her something.

"Quite, Miss Mountford," replied Jepson tactfully, leaving the room.

'Oh, bother,' she cursed to herself, 'he is so loyal to Lord Winterton, I should not have expected him to divulge anything.'

Feeling sad she locked up the desk and put the cover on the typewriter.

"I shall return on Friday," she told Jepson. "There are just one or two matters that need my attention and then I shall not be coming back."

"Your wedding is very soon, I believe, miss?"

"Yes, in three weeks," she answered, putting on her driving hat and gloves.

She had driven herself in her new motor car that afternoon.

It had been a present from Edward, who would have preferred to have bought her a horse, but she had insisted on a motor car.

"Then may I offer my very best wishes and congratulations? I will be sorry not to see you at the Manor again and I am certain that his Lordship will as well."

It was on the tip of Lucia's tongue to press him further on his observation, but she simply smiled and picked up her bag from the desk.

As he watched her leave, Jepson walked towards the

telephone in the study.

Picking up the receiver, he waited until the exchange answered.

"Good afternoon, please put me through to the Athenaeum Club – ah, Athenaeum Club? This is Mr. Jepson, Lord Winterton's butler. I wish to leave an urgent message for him."

*

By the time that Friday came, the last thing Lucia wanted to do was to return to Longridge Manor.

Throughout the rest of the week she had given herself a stern talking-to and was doing her best to push Lord Winterton completely out of her mind.

She even had a most pleasant dinner with Edward when she could almost believe herself to be in love with him. He had made a tremendous effort to have his cook prepare her favourite foods and there was champagne on ice.

He then presented her with a poem he had written about her that had almost melted her heart.

And now she found herself, rather reluctantly, in the Rolls Royce with Briggs at the wheel.

"Would you mind waiting for me?" she told him. "I shall not be that long today. I do not intend to stay for more than a few hours."

"You take as long as you like, Miss Mountford. I shall miss our little jaunts out once you are married and I shall also miss the delicious teas at the Manor."

Lucia smiled to herself.

She looked up at the Jacobean exterior as the motor car drew up at the front entrance. She noticed that the roses at the front were beginning to come into bloom and their bright petals stood out starkly against the dark brick of the building.

Moving quickly inside, she took off her hat and gloves.

It was cool inside the hall and she noticed that a large flower arrangement stood on the sideboard.

'How lovely,' she thought. 'I wonder if Jepson had them brought in as he knew this would be my last day here? I must thank him.'

She set about writing the last few letters and checking the arrangements for the ceremony. She knew that Jepson would be expecting her to leave a long list for Lord Winterton plus a schedule for the day.

'Now for the schedule,' mumbled Lucia, feeling quite sad that her duties were almost complete.

She typed up a list of events for the day accompanied by precise instructions.

Next she wrote to the bandmaster, the Mayor and the King's private secretary, leaving copies of the letters for Lord Winterton.

"I can see that you haven't missed me!"

Lucia let out a gasp as there, standing in the doorway, was Lord Winterton.

He looked devastatingly handsome with a bloom of rude health on him. His skin glowed and his eyes shone brightly.

He was obviously delighted to see her.

"Richard!"

She blushed deeply the moment she had let his Christian name slip from her lips. She realised that perhaps she should not have addressed him so familiarly.

"Yes, I have returned," he murmured and then, moving towards her with his hand outstretched, he added, "and may I add my belated congratulations on your forthcoming marriage? I read about it when I was in Vienna – in *The Times*."

Lucia bowed her head as he shook her hand.

"Yes, I assumed you would see the announcement," she muttered, feeling overcome with emotion. "You are not angry with me?"

"For breaking the deal I had forged with your stepfather? No, I had expected such a thing might come to pass in my absence. Now, I am glad I have caught you – we should get down to work at once. Shall I ask Jepson to make certain that your driver is made comfortable? He may be here longer than you had anticipated."

There was a different air about Lord Winterton – something Lucia could not quite explain. He seemed quieter and less brash. Even his body movements were slower and less strident.

'Something has happened to him, but what?' she thought, as she tried to still her beating heart.

It was immensely difficult having him so close to her, when all she wanted to do was have him take her in his arms.

"Your mother, she is better?"

"Almost completely recovered," replied Lucia. "Thanks to your doctor. I am afraid that I will be on honeymoon when the ceremony happens, but Mama has said that she will gladly take my place."

"And I was heartened, too, to hear of your stepfather's good fortune. Diamond mines in South Africa, is it not? It was very good of him to repay the debt so promptly and with interest. There was no need for him to do that."

"Stepfather likes to do things in a business-like fashion," commented Lucia, trying not to meet his burning blue gaze.

'It is as if another man has inhabited his body!' conjectured Lucia, as they went through the schedule together.

An hour later they had come to the end of their tasks and Lord Winterton rose from his chair.

"Thank you for everything," he said in a low voice. "It was a great deal of work to leave you with and I am sorry that I ran off like that."

"It was nothing and you forget that I have a vested interest in the project as Papa is also being commemorated."

"I trust that the stonemason has done us proud?"

"Yes, very much so. The likeness is incredible and so very dignified."

"Good, I am so pleased. Look, Lucia – "

"Sir, please – " she protested.

Her heart was now beating incredibly fast as he had moved closer to her.

His expression was both intense and earnest as he towered over her.

"No, let me explain. I owe you an apology," he began. "I ran off to Austria without leaving word, but I could not tell a soul what I was doing as I was acting on behalf of the King.

"As I am sure you know, there is trouble in that part of the world and my mission was highly secret. I know that there was all kind of wild speculation about my sudden disappearance and the meddling of a certain lady of my acquaintance only served as a convenient distraction to what was really going on."

Lucia looked at him. What she wanted to say to him dried on her lips as hope sprang anew in her heart.

"Do you mean that you were not with Lady Shelley – and that the story I read in the *Westminster Gazette* – was false?" she stuttered.

Lord Winterton sighed heavily and moved even nearer. So close, in fact, that Lucia could feel his warmth. How she longed to reach out to him and to touch him!

"It was," he replied, "and I have cut off all dealings with her as a result. She mistakenly thought I would marry her and so contacted the paper in question with the story in order to push me into a proposal."

"How devious!" gasped Lucia. "But she always did give the impression that she was a woman who was used to getting whatever she wanted."

"Quite so, but on this occasion, she failed. She should have known me better than to try to entrap me. The truth is that – "

"I am sorry to interrupt, my Lord, but there is an urgent telephone call for you."

Lucia saw a surge of anger light up Lord Winterton's eyes. He seemed highly irritated that he had been interrupted.

"Dammit, man, tell them I will call them back!"

"But it is His Majesty's Office at Buckingham Palace," replied Jepson in an insistent tone.

"Lucia, I am sorry, we shall have to continue this conversation another time. But continue it we shall, I promise you. And before it's too late – "

With that, he threw her a look that made her tremble.

'Oh, curse Jepson and curse the King! Why did he have to come in at that precise moment?' she muttered, as she left the Manor. 'What was he going to say to me? I cannot bear it! I know what I desire in my heart, but am I simply fooling myself?'

She stared out of the window of the Rolls Royce as it sped down the drive.

'Please say that you love me,' she cried, as she imagined him on the telephone behind the walls of Longridge Manor. '*Rescue me*! Come and get me, I beg you!'

CHAPTER TEN

The next few weeks were a blur for Lucia. There was so much to do and she felt as if her head was constantly spinning.

She also found herself becoming increasingly irritated by Edward as the days sped by and still there was no word from Lord Winterton.

'What did I expect?' she told herself, crossly, as she gazed out of the window of the drawing room.

She was awaiting the arrival of the dressmaker who was coming all the way from Bond Street for the final fitting of her wedding dress.

"If that girl sticks pins in me, I shall scream at the top of my voice!" threatened Lucia, as her mother entered the room.

"Darling, I wanted to have a word with you as you seem so very tense. I know we have spoken before about pre-wedding nerves, but last night you really upset Edward."

Lucia felt ashamed of herself. It was true, she had been perfectly vile to Edward during dinner the previous evening.

He had made some comment about how he preferred her hair longer and hoped that she was not going to cut it after they were married, and Lucia had rounded on him, telling him that if she wanted to shave it off like a convict, then she would.

Even Sir Arthur had commented upon her waspish retort.

Poor Edward had looked punctured and, in spite of attempting to explain his casual remark as being a mere preference, rather than an order, he had not been able to prevent Lucia from snapping at him every time he said something.

In the end she had stormed off to bed and cried herself to sleep.

She was ashamed of herself for having behaved so abominably, but she recognised she was fighting a losing battle with her feelings for Lord Winterton.

She thought of him constantly and even attempted to find an excuse to return to Longridge Manor.

"But you have ceased to work for him," her mother had said, half fearing what her daughter's irritable response might be.

"I just thought that perhaps I should run through the schedule with him once more for the day of the unveiling."

"Darling, I am perfectly capable of handling whatever might happen on the day. I am no longer an invalid and my brain was never affected by my illness."

"But I want to make certain that all is well with His Majesty. Just one telephone call to his private secretary that is all I need to do."

"Then, you can just as easily make it from here," replied her mother. "I do not think it is right to go careering over to another gentleman's house, when you are engaged to Edward. It gives the wrong impression."

Lucia knew that her mother was right. People would think it strange that she was not fully occupied with her wedding preparations.

"Besides," she added, "Mrs. de Redcliffe and her chef are coming tomorrow to bring samples of food for the wedding breakfast. You simply must be here to receive them."

"Naturally," she conceded, wishing that the whole lot of them would disappear in a puff of smoke.

At eleven o'clock on the dot, Madame Joy and her entourage arrived at Bingham Hall in a great flurry of boxes and material.

"Mademoiselle Mountford – ah, I think you 'ave lost weight yet again," sighed Madame Joy, as she entered the drawing room, closely followed by Moston and their new footman carrying several large boxes.

"You look so pale. Zis is not right!" chattered Madame Joy. "You must eat ze beef steak and ze liver."

Lucia glanced at her reflection in the large gilt-framed mirror that hung over the white marble fireplace.

It was true, she had lost weight and there were dark circles under her eyes. The result of too many nights staring into the darkness, thinking of Lord Winterton and hoping that he would ride up to Bingham Hall and rescue her from the wedding.

"Come, you must put on ze dress," urged Madame Joy, as she unpacked the gorgeous white silk dress with its cream-coloured lace.

Standing on a chair, the skirt was straight and fell from Lucia's hips like a sheath, whilst the bodice was fitted with long sleeves and a high neck.

"Oof!" cried Madame Joy. "Zat is another inch to be taken in on ze waist."

"Darling, I know you want to look your best on your wedding day," came in her mother, "but Edward does not want his new wife to be a bag of bones!"

As they fussed around her, Lucia's mind strayed to Lord Winterton again.

'I was wrong about him,' she told herself, as the dressmaker pushed and pulled at her. 'Whatever secret business he is engaged upon on behalf of the King explains why he appeared as if he was gadding about. Of course, he could not tell me what it was and his louche behaviour provided him with the perfect cover.'

"Please, mademoiselle, you must stand still."

Lucia tried to stare straight ahead, but she found it irritating being pulled around and today, she was not at all in the mood.

'It's no good – I am in love with him,' she sighed, 'and now it is too late. He's not coming for me, I am to be married in four days and then I shall never see him again."

"Mademoiselle, please!" exclaimed Madame Joy impatiently. "It is important we get ze bodice right!"

It was all too much for Lucia. All at once the dam of her emotions broke like a flood and she burst into tears, sobbing noisily as she stood on the chair.

"Will you please leave us?" asked her mother somewhat alarmed.

She shooed Madame Joy out and closed the door.

"Darling. What on earth is it?" she said, helping her down from the chair and out of the dress.

"Oh, Mama. I am so miserable." cried Lucia, her face wet with tears.

Her mother helped her to the sofa and gave her a handkerchief.

"This is more than pre-wedding nerves," she counselled quietly. "Darling, whatever it is, can you not confide in me? This should be the happiest time of your life and yet you seem so unhappy."

"Oh, Mama, I am not in love with Edward," she confessed, blurting out the words in a torrent of yet more tears.

"Is that all? Oh, don't be silly, Lucia. Plenty of women are not in love with their husbands on their wedding day, but have wonderful marriages. Perhaps love will grow?"

"No, Mama," bawled Lucia, wringing the handkerchief. "It will not."

"But when the children come along, you will feel differently. You will love him for giving you such a precious gift, I promise you."

"*I will not!*" cried Lucia defiantly. "Because I am in love with someone else!"

There was an awful silence while her mother thought. She put her arm around Lucia's shoulders and pulled her close. She let her cry noisily on her bosom for a few moments and then spoke as gently as she could.

"Then, you must tell Edward and put off the wedding. We will not mind. Your stepfather is a changed man since the turn in his fortunes and will understand. Does this other man love you?"

"I have no idea!" sobbed Lucia. "Oh, Mama! What shall I do?"

"If you really think that you cannot go through with this wedding, then you must tell Edward at once. And as for the man you love – does he know this?"

Lucia felt even more miserable as she shook her head and inhaled the comforting scent of lavender from her mother's dress.

She let out an audible sigh and let Lucia go.

"It's Lord Winterton, is it not?"

Lucia looked at her with a shocked expression.

However had she guessed?

"Oh, Mama! It's hopeless! He does not love me – I know he doesn't. No, the wedding will go ahead with Edward. I am being perfectly foolish and am just a little over-tired. I have not been sleeping well and I am just so very nervous."

"Oh, my darling, I had suspected as much. Oh, *that man*!"

"It's not his fault. He has not made me fall in love with him," replied Lucia, quickly springing to his defence. "It's just that I have never met anyone like him before, so handsome, so dashing, so – well, manly!"

"He is certainly that, I grant you," agreed her mother a little tartly.

"No, Mama, I will marry Edward and I shall endeavour to stop this utter foolishness. Send the dressmaker away – I shall go for a long ride to clear my head."

"If you are certain, dearest – "

"Yes, Mama. Now go and relay my apologies to Madame Joy."

Lucia heard voices in the corridor and waited until the front door closed before she walked out into the hall.

Running upstairs, she made for her bedroom, hoping that her riding habit would be close to hand. It was right at the front of the wardrobe and she pulled it down eagerly. She found her boots and gloves and quickly changed.

Before long she was heading for the stables feeling measurably brighter.

'It is a while since I last rode out on my own,' she mused, as she hailed Jack and asked him to have Flash saddled at once.

She waited impatiently while the horse was made

ready and could not wait to mount. He was one of Sir Arthur's most recent acquisitions and Lucia had been longing to ride him.

"Come on, boy!" she urged, digging her heels into his side.

Flash sped off across the fields behind the Hall and soon they were riding across the ridge that ran along the edge of the estate.

The cool breeze soothed Lucia and the warm sun made her feel much better. It was a fine July day and reminded her of everything good about an English summer.

After a while, Lucia could tell that Flash was thirsty and she had not brought a bottle of water with her.

"Shall we head for the river, boy?" she called, as they paused by a field.

The horse whinnied and Lucia turned him to the right.

"Then we shall go this way!" she cried, urging him onwards.

It was a long gallop downhill to the river and the sun beat down mercilessly. At last, they reached it and, gratefully, Lucia slid down off Flash's back and led him to the water's edge.

She let the horse drink, while she cupped her hands in the cool water and quenched her own thirst. The water tasted sweet and cool and she dangled her hands into the current as it hurried downstream.

It was then that she realised that she had brought her horse to the exact place where Lord Winterton had attempted to kiss her.

She shielded her eyes from the sun's rays as she picked out the dusty turning where she had left the car and the dirt road beyond.

'It all seems so long ago,' she sighed, 'and now, I am

to be married in a few days time.'

She sat down on the grass while Flash continued to sink his nose into the bubbling water.

"You are very thirsty, aren't you?" she said, laughing at him.

Beads of sweat stood out on his fine chestnut hide and she wondered if she should flick some water over him. To her amusement, Flash stepped straight into the river, allowing the water to foam around his hooves.

Just as she was enjoying his frolics, she heard the sounds of another horse's hooves coming towards them.

Squinting in the direction of the sound, the sun dazzled her eyes and at first she could not make out who the approaching rider might be.

"Your horse has the right idea."

"Richard!" she murmured. "It's Lord Winterton!"

She jumped up and ran to meet him. His horse was panting hard and tossing its head.

"I thought I would find you here. Your mother said you would most likely be by the river."

"Mama – ?"

He dismounted and let his horse wander off towards the bank.

Gently he took Lucia's hands in his and kissed them.

"No, you must not – " she reacted, willing him not to stop.

He gazed into her eyes and pulled her closer.

"Lucia – *dearest Lucia.*"

Lucia's heart hammered in her chest as she once again thrilled to his touch.

His expression was so full of emotion that she could scarcely bear to meet his eyes.

"I realise that I have probably left this too late," he began, "but if I do not tell you now, then I may never have another chance."

"What is it?" she asked softly. "You know I am to be married on Saturday."

"I know, and that is why I have made haste to find you today. Lucia, the truth is that I love you. When I was in Austria, I could do nothing but think of you and, then, I read the announcement and realised that I had probably lost my chance.

"I never intended to hold your stepfather to our bargain. It was a careless remark that he took far too seriously and then it seemed fun to continue the charade and to have you at the Manor as my secretary. I would never marry a woman against her will. What must you have thought of me?"

"That you were not of good character," replied Lucia, returning his intense gaze. "And then there was Lady Shelley acting as if she was your wife, when her own husband had not long been cold in his grave."

"I can see that you have heard the gossip about me and I confess that Lady Shelley and I were entangled for a while. But no longer – "

"She is a very determined woman, Richard."

"And I can only apologise for her behaviour and mine. I should have nipped it in the bud a good deal earlier but, as you so wisely point out, she is very determined. But you should have no fears as neither of us will be hearing from her, or seeing her, again. Lucia – "

He paused and squeezed her hand, entreating her earnestly with his eyes.

"Lucia, I know you do not love me – "

"But I do," interrupted Lucia, looking up at him with

her heart overflowing. "*I do*. More than anything."

"Is this true? Do you really love me after how dreadfully I have behaved towards you?" he asked gently.

"*I love you so very much*," she murmured.

Lord Winterton did not hesitate. He put his arms around her and, tilting her head towards his, his mouth met hers in a long lingering kiss.

Lucia was in Heaven and she felt as if someone had given her the sun, moon and stars all at once.

Her heart soared as their lips parted, but still, he held her close.

"What can we do, my darling?" he asked her urgently, as they stood together, locked in an embrace. "On Saturday, you are marrying Edward de Redcliffe and *I want you to marry me*. You know that, don't you?"

Lucia looked down at her hands, nestling on his chest – her mouth a firm and resolute line.

"Now, I know what I have to do. Richard, I will marry you and I cannot marry him. It's as simple as that. In fact, I almost called off the wedding this morning as I realised that I was in love with you, but then, I did not believe that you could feel the same way for me.

"Will you come back to Bingham Hall with me? There is a very important telephone call I have to make."

"Surely, you are not going to break off your engagement over the telephone?"

"No, my darling. But I will ask him to come over straight away. Edward is a very resolute man. He wants a wife far more than he wants me and he will find another candidate within a month, I promise you."

With joy in his heart, Lord Winterton embraced her in his strong arms and then kissed her once more.

"Say again that you will marry me."

"*Yes*," she answered, looking up into his brilliant blue eyes so full of love for her.

Jumping back on their horses, the pair of them rode like the wind to Bingham Hall. Leaving their mounts at the stables, they ran hand-in-hand inside.

Her mother was waiting for them and she ushered Lord Winterton into the drawing room while Lucia went straight to the telephone.

After a few moments she came in, her face drained of all colour.

"Well?" asked Lord Winterton, jumping up as she entered the room.

"He was very quiet and very sensible, but he says he is on his way here to discuss the matter. Richard, I think it would be best if you returned home. I shall telephone you later and tell you what has happened."

"If that is what you want, my dearest Lucia."

She accompanied him as far as the front door. He kissed her tenderly and promised that he would be waiting to hear from her.

'Now all I have to do is break off my engagement,' sighed Lucia, as she returned to the drawing room and her mother.

*

Edward was exceedingly pale when he arrived at Bingham Hall. Moston ushered him into the drawing room where Lucia was waiting for him alone.

Her mother had told Moston that she would be in the morning room and to send for her immediately if there was any trouble.

"Edward," said Lucia in a low voice as he entered the room.

"Lucia."

153

"Edward, I believe you know what I am going to say. I think my behaviour of the past few weeks has alerted you to the fact that all is not well between us."

She looked towards him for a reply, but found him mute and so she continued with the speech she had prepared.

"The fact is that I am in love with someone else and he loves me too. Edward, I cannot marry you. I am so sorry and I think it would be best if we broke off our engagement at once."

She pulled the emerald ring from her finger and handed it to him. He took it, looked at it for a second and then closed his fist around it.

"I will have my man send urgent telegrams to all my family and friends," said Edward stiffly. "I trust you will see to the other arrangements?"

"Naturally," replied Lucia, relieved that he had taken the news so calmly.

Edward rose from his chair and took a deep breath.

"I cannot say that this has been a complete shock, as I had realised that things were out of sorts. But I trust we can be friends?"

"Of course and I really am very sorry to cause you such hurt. Really I am."

Without making a comment, Edward nodded his head and held out his hand.

"Goodbye, Lucia. Good luck."

"Thank you. I do wish you well and hope you find happiness."

He pursed his lips and left the room.

Lucia sank back down in her chair and felt completely drained as her mother came hurrying in.

"Well?"

"He took it incredibly well. He even wished me good

luck!"

"He is a decent man. And now, I suppose I shall have to cancel everything. Did he say anything else?"

"He said he would inform his family and friends."

"Oh dear. Well, let's not think about it anymore and I expect you will wish to telephone Lord Winterton and tell him the news. Tomorrow, we shall start cancelling all the arrangements and I am afraid that your stepfather will have to bear the cost."

"Does Stepfather know?"

"Yes, I have told him. He was, as I had suspected, quite tolerant of your decision. He wants to see you happy as much as I do."

"You are right. He is a changed man and I would have thought he would be most displeased. In fact, because he had not come storming in, shouting at me, I had thought you had yet to tell him."

Her mother laughed and gently took Lucia's hand.

"Darling. I know that you two got off on the wrong foot together, but he is a good man. I would not have married him otherwise."

Lucia telephoned Lord Winterton at once and informed him that Edward had taken the news quite well.

He said that he would have his driver bring him over to the Hall at once.

"I need to speak with your stepfather as soon as possible. You have not cancelled the Church yet, have you?"

"No, I have not."

"Good," replied Lord Winterton mysteriously.

An hour later, he arrived at the Hall in his Talbot. Lucia ran out to greet him and kissed him as soon as he emerged from the motor car.

"Darling. I have missed you," she cried, taking his

arm.

"I have only been gone a few hours – it's not possible!" he teased.

"Shall I ask Mama and Stepfather to join us?" she suggested, as they settled down on the sofa in the drawing room.

"Yes, I would speak with them at once. We do not have any time to lose."

"What do you mean?"

"I mean, that you are not to cancel anything until I have spoken to your stepfather. Darling, you can still be a bride on Saturday, that is, if you desire it."

Lucia's heart jumped for joy.

"Oh, Richard! Nothing could excite me more! Why should we wait until everything is in place?"

Five minutes later, Sir Arthur and her mother joined them and Lucia quickly informed them that Lord Winterton wished to speak to them alone.

Closing the door behind her, she waited in the hall.

Then the door to the drawing room burst open and Sir Arthur stood there with a huge smile on his face.

"Well!" he exclaimed. "I confess I am somewhat surprised at this turn of events, but if you are happy, my dear, then so am I."

"He has asked for my hand?" asked Lucia tentatively.

"He has and I have agreed," replied Sir Arthur. "I must say, when I saw that story in the *Westminster Gazette*, I simply thought that the man was a bounder. Now he has explained everything to me, I can see I was wrong to believe cheap gossip."

"And the wedding?"

"It can go ahead as planned. I do not see any sense in incurring more expense if you are intending to get married in any case. *The sooner – the better!*"

Lucia ran into the drawing room to find her mother chatting warmly with Lord Winterton.

"Darling," she called, as her face lit up. "I am so very pleased for you. Now, I will leave you two alone as I am certain you have plenty to discuss."

The doors to the garden had been opened and a warm evening breeze blew in. Lord Winterton took her hand and led her out through them.

"Come," he smiled.

Outside they stood in the gardens beneath a rising moon.

The sky was as clear as a bell and everywhere stars twinkled over their heads.

"I will need to go and see Canon Bennett at once to tell him what is happening. It will mean a special licence, but I am not without my influence in the County and should be able to obtain the necessary permission tomorrow."

"Oh, darling, are we really to be married on Saturday? It seems so impossible."

He pulled her close and kissed the soft hair above her forehead.

"Darling, this is not a dream – this is real. We are to be man and wife."

"But you will want to invite your own guests and there is so little time."

"I would not care if it was just you and I at the altar, as long as Canon Bennett will marry us. Darling, I do not want to wait another week, let alone another month, for you to become my wife. I have wasted too much time already. All I ask is that we wait until after the unveiling ceremony before we go on honeymoon. Dearest, would you mind too much?"

"Of course not," she murmured, nuzzling his chest.

She felt so safe and protected close to him.

"With Papa's name inscribed on the monument, it was going to cause me a great deal of distress not to see it revealed in all its glory. In fact, I had only agreed to the date of the honeymoon with Edward in order to avoid seeing you. That was when I thought you were about to marry Lady Shelley."

"My dear sweet silly girl!" he exclaimed, laughing and pulling her close to his lips. "Could you not guess how much I loved you?"

As they kissed, Lucia felt as if she was being carried up to the stars with happiness. She gave herself up to his insistent mouth and became overwhelmed with love for him.

Drawing back from him, the moon's rays bathed them in a glorious silvery light.

"Pinch me, Richard! I think I must be dreaming. How could I be so happy?" she asked, smiling up at him.

With a fond chuckle he took her soft cheek in his fingers and nipped it gently.

"There, my darling, *you are not dreaming*, this is a dream come true."

Lucia pouted with an alarmed look on her face.

"But dreams come to an end and I do not want this one ever to end. I have never had such a perfect moment and if I thought it was just a dream, I would be distraught!"

Lord Winterton turned his face towards her. The moon and stars shone down on them as they kissed once more, basking in God's Love – the most perfect and sublime of all.

"Not this dream, my darling," he sighed, tightening his grip around her. "This one will last forever and ever, I promise you with all my heart and soul."